Why I Would Have Killed Jesus and You Might Have Too

Dear John,

It's been a joy sharing meals with you & Katy in Austin. Best wishes!

Blessings,

~Dave~

10-12-21

Why I Would Have Killed Jesus and You Might Have Too

FIVE SHORT STORIES OF FAITH

David Nelson

RESOURCE *Publications* • Eugene, Oregon

WHY I WOULD HAVE KILLED JESUS AND YOU MIGHT HAVE TOO
Five Short Stories of Faith

Resource Publications
An Imprint of Wipf and Stock Publishers
199 W. 8th Ave., Suite 3
Eugene, OR 97401

www.wipfandstock.com

PAPERBACK ISBN: 978-1-6667-1156-1
HARDCOVER ISBN: 978-1-6667-1157-8
EBOOK ISBN: 978-1-6667-1158-5

Contents

Acknowledgments

THIS BOOK IS THE result of hundreds of conversations stretching many years. I'm especially thankful to Kathy Nelson, The Rt. Rev. C. Andrew Doyle, Jimmy Hemphill, George Ebert, Carol Martin, The Rev. Albert "Bertie" Pearson, Barry Rought, The Rev. Terry Miller, Jonathan Payne, Deb Tisch, Grant Miller, and Robert Stegall. Special thanks to my editor, Dr. Joya Stevenson, who went above and beyond every step of this journey.

I couldn't have finished this book without the support of my amazing wife, The Rev. Beth Anne Nelson. Her ideas, listening ear, and patience are great blessings to me. Finally, to my daughters Grace and Faith, who remind me of God's grace and faith each day.

Introduction

I WOKE UP IN a cold sweat after having the weirdest dream. I had met five strangers from biblical times: a young widow, a fisherman, a grandmother, a soldier, and a religious man. Each one told a dramatic story about a common enemy: Jesus of Nazareth. I saw the events unfolding before my eyes. Their vivid stories were so compelling and persuasive. Worst of all, none of them had horns or a pitchfork. Instead, these enemies of Jesus dominated my imagination precisely because they were so ordinary. They reminded me of my friends, family members, and even myself. That is what made the dream so scary.

As I collected my thoughts, it hit me. The previous day had been Palm Sunday, a day when church members reenact the final week of the life of Jesus. The congregation shouts, "Crucify him! Crucify him!"[1] That's why I dreamed about his death and the people who hated him. That certainly explained the dream, but my nightmare had just begun.

I'm a priest, so loving and serving Jesus is the foundation of my life. Yet I encounter him from the comfortable perch of 2,000 years of hindsight. This dream shattered my complacency by bringing me back to the time and place of Jesus and forcing me to consider many uncomfortable points of view. I tried to forget the dream, but those pesky voices, the voices of his opponents, would not stop nagging me. They insisted I listen to their side of the story, haunting me with a terrifying possibility. Had I walked a mile in their shoes—or, more accurately, sandals—I would have acted as they did. I would have killed Jesus too.

"Surely not I, Lord?"[2] I balked. Yet this was the same protest the disciples offered before leaving Jesus for dead. I pondered how thousands witnessed his ministry in action, while only a few stuck with him to the bitter end. I grew so exhausted from this struggle with God over my own complicity that I decided to write down all five accounts.

What follows are five short stories told by each character from my dream. The language came to me in our modern tongue, so the words will feel familiar. Each story delves into various biblical scenes, historical conflicts, and theological controversies from the gospels. The characters present points of view that are consistent with the cultural and historical realities of the time of Jesus. They include plausible biblical interpretations and accurate knowledge of the Holy Land. These stories cite Scripture frequently, always correctly quoting Jesus word for word. Of course, there are fictional twists, imaginative turns, and dramatic retellings of the biblical narratives. Minor biblical characters are provided with developed backstories, and these five storytellers are imaginary; they exist only in my dreams. Like many stories and dreams, this one weaves fact and fiction together so convincingly that I am still trying to separate the two.

Now, let's meet all five characters. The first chapter introduces Deborah of Bethany, a young widow eager to throw off the shackles of the violent Roman occupation. A disciple of Jesus and a courageous warrior, she stands ready for battle. In the second chapter we meet Shem of Capernaum, a fisherman with a passion for helping leaders attract and keep crowds. He hopes to grow a bigger crowd while Jesus keeps driving them away. In the third chapter we encounter Sarah of Nazareth, a protective grandmother from his childhood home. She warns her grandchildren about Jesus, especially his dangerous love for Israel's enemies. She also recounts the horrible day when he enraged the good people of the synagogue in Nazareth. The fourth chapter introduces Maximus Gallus, an obedient Roman soldier, who is committed to law and order. He grows irritated by the rebellious teachings of Jesus, which cause conflict between him and his military superior. In the fifth chapter we meet Aaron of Arimathea, a troubled young man who finds his path as a religious leader, a Pharisee. He is inspired by the love of Jesus yet offended by his apparent disregard for Scripture. These stories are followed by a short conclusion.

This book is subtitled "Five Short Stories of Faith" because all five storytellers are people of faith who came into conflict with Jesus. I urge you to consider these accounts charitably, with empathy and compassion, or, as Jesus put it, to "love your enemies."[3] Perhaps one way to love the enemies of Jesus is to listen to their stories.

Rather than explain away the book title with a list or analysis, I offer these stories, which are like extended parables, as my answer. In their stories I see reflections of my own heart. I invite you to search your heart and make similar connections. While these characters are set in ancient times, consider where you see them in our modern world. You may be disturbed to discover that you can be an enemy of Jesus too. Dare to love your enemies, because in doing so you may also be loving yourself.

I share the message of my dream, which prompted this book, together with an urgent warning: if you treasure a safe, meek, and mild image of Jesus, please do not read any further. These five stories are meant to provoke an encounter with Jesus like never before—through the eyes of his enemies.

CHAPTER I

Deborah of Bethany

MY NAME IS DEBORAH of Bethany. I am a young widow, fighting to topple the corrupt Romans. This passion led me to a fierce revolutionary named Jesus of Nazareth. I followed him until I discovered he did not possess a warrior spirit, nor did he establish a new kingdom. He accepted the ruthless Roman occupation and refused to fight against our terrible oppressors.

I grew up in a village called Bethany, which is just outside of Jerusalem. I'm the youngest of four children, two girls and two boys. My parents always recognized my courage and my intellectual gifts. I can't explain it, but I can hear Scripture read once and never forget it.

My father was a master storyteller, and the subject was always the great heroes of Israel. At bedtime he would ask us, "Kids, who will the Messiah be like?" Upon hearing this familiar question, we would shout the names of various biblical heroes. For example, when my brother said, "The Messiah will be like King David," my father replied, "That's exactly right. King David was once just a humble shepherd boy who fought against a mighty Philistine named Goliath. He trusted in the Lord and bravely defeated the giant with a slingshot. While that may have been his first battle, it wasn't his last. David grew up and became king, uniting the twelve tribes of Israel. He fought against the wicked King Saul and endured the betrayal of his son, Absalom. Yes, children, when the

Messiah comes, he will be like David. He will be a descendant of David, who comes from humble origins and rises to become king, and this warrior will reestablish the twelve tribes of Israel."

Another night my father asked us, "Kids, who will the Messiah be like?"

"The Messiah will be like Moses," my sister replied.

"That's exactly right," my father said. "Moses grew angry under the brutal Egyptians, who enslaved his people. When he saw an Egyptian mercilessly beating a poor Israelite, Moses courageously stood up to that tyrant, killing him to save an innocent life. Later, the Lord heard the cries of our people and sent Moses to confront Pharaoh, saying, 'Let my people go.'⁴ When Pharaoh refused, the Lord used Moses to lead our people out of Egypt with his mighty hand, parting the Red Sea. As the Egyptian army pursued, the waters returned and destroyed them all. Moses freed our people from slavery. After their escape from Egypt, the Lord led them to the wilderness. God gave the commandments to Moses at Mount Sinai, and those laws continue to guide us today.

"Yes, children," he concluded, "the Messiah will be a courageous leader who will free us from oppression. He will be a wise teacher of the commandments too."

I began to cry as my father finished speaking. He took me aside. "What's wrong, Deborah?" he asked.

"Father, I want to be a mighty warrior," I said. "But I can't be like David or Moses because I'm just a girl."

"Oh, Deborah." He shook his head while consoling me. "Silly child, you don't understand what you are saying. Listen carefully; this is the story of how you got your name."

Then he told me the incredible story.

"Deborah was a prophetess and a judge of Israel. Meanwhile, the evil king of Canaan, Jabin, overtook her people. The Canaanites had more military power than anyone could imagine—nine hundred iron chariots! Nobody thought the Israelites could win—except Deborah. She summoned a man named Barak to command them into battle, but he was afraid to fight without the mighty Deborah's assurance. She knew the Lord would deliver victory.

Sure enough, they wiped out every last Canaanite. Israel fought a revolution and won, thanks to the heroism of a warrior prophetess named Deborah."

I jumped up and down. "So girls can be warriors too?"

"Anything is possible with God," my father affirmed. "When your mother was pregnant, you kicked her so much, she knew you had a restless spirit. When the time came, you almost didn't survive, but you fought like a warrior. I thought for certain you were a boy. When your mother held you in her arms, we rejoiced that the Lord gave us a daughter with such a warrior spirit, just like Deborah. Never forget this story. This is who you are."

I am Deborah, a warrior with a fierce spirit. My father's stories have shaped me into the person I am. I spent much of my childhood searching for the coming Messiah, a pursuit that others ridiculed. For example, one year our family was in Jerusalem for our annual celebration of Passover. I was with my older brother, Jesse, as we discussed the coming Messiah with a group of children. I hid behind my brother and whispered words into his ear. As Jesse spoke, the children marveled at his wisdom, nicknaming him "Little Solomon."

The children began to ask questions until all eyes were in our direction. I covered my mouth to hide our trick. Eventually, a boy figured out our scheme. They began chanting, "She's a freak. She's a freak."

I burst into tears and ran away. It just wasn't fair. When they thought wisdom came from a boy, they called him Little Solomon. When they discovered this same wisdom came from a girl, they called me a freak. How I yearn to find a place where I belong. I dream of joining fellow warriors ready to fight in the name of the Lord.

When I was of age, I married a man named Daniel, a good man, quiet and strong. We dreamed of the coming revolution. I helped pick out his armor for battle. He loved hearing me talk passionately about the great heroes of Israel.

One day only a month after we were married, my father and my husband went to Jerusalem together while I remained in

Bethany. A woman in town named Mary began telling astonishing stories about her rabbi, Jesus of Nazareth. After the crowds dispersed, I remained, hanging on every word she said.

Mary smiled with delight. "Thanks for listening, Deborah," she said. "People often dismiss my words. They claim that a respectable rabbi would never call a woman to be a disciple. Trust me when I tell you his message is powerful."

"Please tell me more."

Mary's face grew stern with conviction as she spoke. "His message is about the kingdom of God and how things are going to change in a hurry. The exalted will be humbled while the humbled will be exalted. He will bring down the powerful while lifting up the lowly. The poor will receive good news while the rich will be sent away empty-handed. I have never seen anyone speak with such authority."

Mary's words made my heart pound with excitement like never before. My father had told me so many bedtime stories about Israel's heroes. Now the kingdom of God could truly be coming. I quizzed her more. "Where is he from? Do you think he might be a son of David like the prophecies say?"

"Yes! He is a son of David. He was born in Bethlehem and raised in Nazareth," Mary replied, raising her voice in excitement. She looked in my eyes. "You sure have some good questions. I will let you know the next time he is near, so you can meet him yourself."

Mary's amazing words got me thinking. Perhaps the Lord had heard our cries and was preparing us for battle.

Suddenly, my mother came running toward me, wailing with a shriek. "Deborah! Deborah! Oh, it's so bad." My heart was immediately filled with dread. She fell to her knees as people comforted her. "It's Daniel," she said, "and your father. They killed them!"

Those words hit my stomach like a mighty punch. I fell to my knees and cried like never before. I knew who had murdered them. It had to be the Romans.

Soon, I learned the grisly details. It happened in Jerusalem. There was a scuffle between a Roman soldier and a group of Jews.

The soldier nearly beat a poor old man to death. While most on-lookers were silent in the face of this great injustice, my father bravely spoke up, like when Moses confronted the Egyptian. "You have no right to do this," he said. "The days are coming when the God of Israel will raise up a Messiah. He will be a mighty warrior who will defeat tyrants like you."

The soldier scoffed. "I have every right to do this. This land, all of this, belongs to Lord Caesar. Where is this God of Israel? I don't see him anywhere!" He laughed, taking pleasure in mocking my father as well as the Lord.

Daniel bravely joined my father's side. Meanwhile, a group of soldiers formed a circle around them. When one jerked a spear toward my father's face, out of instinct, my father reached for a knife to defend himself. The soldiers pounced like lions devouring a lamb, piercing my father and Daniel with their spears. They murdered them both—for what?

I was so numb that I couldn't sleep for days. Mary came to console us. After she left, I told my mother, "These Romans have got to go. They murder, humiliate, and mock us. I know the Lord hears our prayers. The pain I am feeling is far worse than what our ancestors felt in Egypt. We need to break free from this horrid oppression.

"While these are dark days, there may be hope for us. Moments before you told me the horrible news, I was speaking with Mary. She told me about a man who comes from humble origins, like King David. He's from Nazareth, and that's about as humble as it gets. What if he's the king to bring about the revolution promised in Scripture? He's preaching nearby soon. Will you join me when I go to listen to him?"

My mother teared up, speaking with a heavy heart. "Deborah, you are brave and smart. You have a spark of light in your eyes. Your father and Daniel would want you to do this. While my spirit is so broken that I can hardly breathe, I take comfort in being near you. I will go with you."

The next day we traveled to meet Jesus. After struggling through a large crowd, we found him. He spoke with great passion and authority, just as Mary had promised. He healed many sick people, restored sight to a blind man, and taught with wisdom greater than Solomon. I had never seen anything like it. Then he spoke words I will never forget: "I came to bring fire to the earth . . . Do you think that I have come to bring peace to the earth? No, I tell you, but rather division!"[5]

How I had yearned to hear such powerful words. Jesus was eager to bring change. He knew that peace couldn't be accomplished without a revolution. Fire and division had to come first. My mother and I joined his mission and gladly became his disciples.

Jesus was exactly what I was looking for, a fierce and passionate leader. He had a tender side too. He always said the right words at the right time. I found healing in this teaching of his, "Come to me, all you that are weary and are carrying heavy burdens, and I will give you rest."[6]

My mother found strength in these words of his, "Blessed are those who mourn, for they will be comforted."[7] Our hearts were renewed by his life-giving wisdom.

Jesus told many incredible stories, quickly gaining disciples for his revolution. He refused to give up on anyone. He welcomed lepers, tax collectors, and even prostitutes. He inspired all of them to cling to hope. Despite losing nearly everything, I found new life and hope through him.

One day Jesus and his twelve apostles were traveling near the Jordan River. Meanwhile, my mother and I were home in Bethany for a few days of rest. Mary ran to my house and shouted, "Lazarus is sick! He needs help!"

I ran to their home and saw his pale, nearly lifeless body. He would not last long. Before I could open my mouth, Mary and her sister Martha said the same words simultaneously: "We need Jesus."

"I'll take care of it. Just stay with your brother," I declared. I found a couple of messengers and sent instructions on behalf of the sisters. Jesus was to come to Bethany immediately. Seeing the fierceness in my eyes, they hurried on their way.

I returned to pray with the family and console Mary. "Fortunately, Jesus will leap like a lamb and be in Bethany soon," I said. "I hope he arrives by sunset tomorrow." I prayed with the family all night, refusing to sleep.

As I watched Lazarus approach death, I finally had to look away. The grief hit me in the stomach, causing me to feel sick. I stepped outside the home, bent over in pain. Moments later, he was dead. Soon his body was taken away, prepared for burial, and placed in a tomb. Many people came to console the family. Finding one of the messengers, I snarled, "Where is Jesus?"

"I gave him the message exactly as you instructed," he insisted sheepishly. "He should have been here by now."

Lazarus was dead and Jesus was nowhere to be found.

"If only, if only . . ." Mary muttered as I sat with the sisters.

Martha grew angry. She did have a temper, which was understandable given the circumstances. Martha stormed off to confront him. "Lord, if you had been here," she said, "my brother would not have died."[8]

When she returned to Bethany, she seemed different. She approached her sister and pointed to the road. "The Teacher is here and is calling for you."[9]

As Mary hustled to meet him, many mourners joined her. Most of them thought she was going to the tomb of Lazarus until she passed by and continued down the road. As we followed, Jesus finally arrived. Mary knelt at his feet with anguish written on her face. I embraced my mother as we wept together.

"Lord," Mary said, "if you had been here, my brother would not have died."[10]

Jesus was noticeably shaken by his death.

"See how he loved him!"[11] some people said. Others who had witnessed him perform miracles were frustrated by his poor timing.

"Could not he who opened the eyes of the blind man have kept this man from dying?"[12]

I somberly headed to the tomb without saying a word. Jesus began to cry as he led the procession. His tears were shed only a stone's throw from the place where I first learned of my husband and father's murder.

"Take away the stone,"[13] he said.

The thought of rolling away that stone was too much for me. My life was already shrouded in death. Martha tried to reason with him. "Lord, already there is a stench because he has been dead four days."[14]

My heart was in knots. Either Jesus had a great plan that I didn't understand, or he had lost his mind.

"Did I not tell you that if you believed, you would see the glory of God?"[15] he asked.

Several men shrugged at the crazy idea of removing the stone, thinking Jesus was joking. Then they received a fierce stare from Jesus, followed by a nod. They began pushing and grunting. Eventually, the large stone budged and rolled away from the mouth of the cave, sending up a cloud of dust. With squinted eyes and outreached hands, the people struggled to focus on the cave opening. Jesus looked toward heaven with confidence and shouted. "Lazarus, come out!"[16]

Following a moment of pregnant silence, a blur appeared in the mouth of the cave. As the dust settled, we dropped our hands and opened our eyes. We saw a sight like no other as a ghostlike figure emerged from the tomb, wrapped in burial clothes. The "ghost" unwrapped the cloth from his face. It was Lazarus, and he was alive!

Our grief turned into awe; our mourning turned to dancing. Not even death could stop Jesus! This miracle revealed that he was a prophet, and hopefully more than a prophet. My mother and I embraced as our hearts soared into heaven.

Later that evening, Mother grabbed my arm firmly. "Deborah," she said, "I'm so excited. I still can't believe what I just saw. I know the Messiah will topple our adversaries like Joshua destroyed the walls of Jericho. He will make our enemies into a footstool, as the Psalms declare. Do you think Jesus might be the One?"

"The Passover is near," I explained confidently. "Yes, I do believe he is the Messiah. This is the perfect time to begin his revolution. Think about how Moses defeated Pharaoh, how young David conquered Goliath, or how Deborah destroyed Jabin and the Canaanite army. Finally, Caesar will perish, and Jesus will be crowned king! There will no longer be a division between heaven and earth. Just as we prayed for the kingdom to come, it will, and peace will be established. People will come to believe that he is the Messiah. Rome doesn't stand a chance!"

Sure enough, the events began unfolding exactly as I predicted. We were joined by large crowds outside of Jerusalem, high up on the Mount of Olives. Jesus rode on a donkey, fulfilling the prophet Zechariah's prediction about the coming Messiah. We all waved palm branches, which is a symbol of victory for Israel. "Hosanna to the Son of David!" many people shouted. "Blessed is the one who comes in the name of the Lord! Hosanna in the highest heaven!"[17] As he rode into Jerusalem, he had a fierce look in his eyes, like a warrior ready for battle.

Next, Jesus went to the Temple. He made a whip of cords and turned over the tables and drove out the money changers. The Temple belongs to God's kingdom, and Jesus was taking it back! Later, he confronted the Sadducees. They may be Jewish, but they are so corrupt. The Sadducees collaborate with the Romans for money and power, shamefully oppressing their own people. They tried to challenge Jesus with Scripture, which was a foolish move. With wit and wisdom, my rabbi humiliated them. "You are wrong because you know neither the Scriptures nor the power of God,"[18] he said. Finally, someone had put them in their place. Words of fire had been ignited, and they struck Jerusalem like a bolt of lightning!

After these events, I began feeling nervous, as I explained to my mother. "In the Scriptures, many revolutions face opposition from within. King David's son, Absalom, betrayed him. Moses had to deal with the failures of his brother, Aaron, while Deborah had the timid Barak. I fear someone could betray him."

That night Jesus and the twelve apostles had a private Passover meal together. It was not until the following morning that we learned what had transpired. One of his closest disciples, Judas Iscariot, had betrayed him. When they came to arrest him, another one of his disciples, Simon Peter, courageously took out his sword and cut the ear off the high priest's slave.

Curiously, Jesus did not seize the moment. Instead, he said, "Put your sword back into its place; for all who take the sword will perish by the sword. Do you think that I cannot appeal to my Father, and he will at once send me more than twelve legions of angels?"[19] Plus, Jesus healed that man's ear. Then they arrested Jesus and took him away in chains.

I turned to my mother. "I'm confused," I said. "Why did he say to put away the sword? If the Lord could win the battle, why not fight at that very moment?"

My mother grasped for an answer. "Maybe he has another plan that we don't understand. After all, Jesus has confused us before, like when he raised Lazarus from the dead."

"Perhaps," I said. "His wisdom can be hard to understand at times. Mother, do you remember when David defeated Goliath?"

"Of course."

"Imagine if David had put down his slingshot and said, 'Those who live by the slingshot, die by the slingshot.' That would have been ridiculous. David had to defeat an evil enemy before he could bring peace. So, why did Jesus tell Simon Peter to put away his sword? I pray for the time to come when we will fight, and time is running out."

"But Jesus said to pray for your enemies."

"Yes, he did say that, Mother," I affirmed. "I agree that we should pray for our enemies. Like it is written in Ecclesiastes, 'For everything there is a season . . .'[20] We must remember the final line of this great poem, '. . . a time for war, and a time for peace.'[21] This is a time for war. We must crush our enemies. Once we win the war, the season of peace can begin. Did Moses confront Pharaoh and say, 'I am praying for you'? Of course not! With a warrior spirit, he stood up to Pharaoh and demanded, 'Let my people go.'[22] While his latest actions seem foolish now, Jesus must have his battle plan ready."

The following morning, we gathered with the crowds and saw many prisoners. The sight of Jesus in chains was heartbreaking, but

I clung to hope. "I think he will miraculously break those chains and slay Pilate," I told my mother. "Now is the time to act."

As we awaited his trial, many in the crowd said there was another revolutionary in town. Rumor had it he was promising victory over the Romans and that he was eager to keep up his work. Oddly, his name was Jesus too, Jesus Barabbas. As we waited, I asked one of his followers about him. "Jesus Barabbas is incredible," he said. "He is powerful and strong like a lion. He will show Pilate who is really in control. That much I know."

Word carried through the crowd that Jesus had told Pilate, "My kingdom is not from this world. If my kingdom were from this world, my followers would be fighting to keep me from being handed over to the Jews."[23] I prayed this was a lie. Yet these words were so similar to what he had said upon his arrest. The tension was too much to bear.

Next, Roman soldiers led my rabbi before Pontius Pilate. The contrast between the two men, both named Jesus, was stark. Barabbas energized the crowd with his charming words. Meanwhile, my teacher looked defeated, his head hanging down, staring at his sandals, not saying a word.

I looked at my mother. "What's happening?" I asked. "This doesn't appear to be the same man. If he doesn't act quickly, he's going to be crucified!"

She had no answer; she just hugged me as the roaring crowds pressed in upon us, chanting, "Release Barabbas for us!"[24] Barabbas was such a commanding presence, ready for action, that Pilate decided to release him to prevent a riot.

What happened next was my worst nightmare. Soldiers whipped Jesus until he fell to the ground, writhing in pain. I fell to my knees in grief as I watched him suffer. Meanwhile, soldiers wove a crown of thorns and slammed it on his head, sending streams of blood dripping down his face. The soldiers laughed in mockery as they bowed at his feet, saying, 'Hail, King of the Jews!'[25] The horror only grew worse when he was led to the cross as people shouted at him to save himself. I understand why. What revolution can take place when the leader is dead?

The twelve apostles were nowhere to be found. I gathered with several women who were weeping. "Why is he letting this happen?" I snarled. "I thought he was the Messiah. Why won't he fight?"

The women just sobbed, saying nothing. Worse yet, Jesus never stopped believing that he was a king leading a revolution.

"Jesus, remember me when you come into your kingdom,"[26] one of the criminals on the cross next to him said.

"Truly I tell you, today you will be with me in Paradise,"[27] he replied.

Those words were the ultimate betrayal. There was no revolution to come. What kind of king wears a crown of thorns? Where is this paradise he promised? I put my heart, mind, and strength into following Jesus. He was supposed to be a warrior sent to free Israel, but he wouldn't even fight. He stood before Pilate and did nothing. Nothing! This man could raise the dead, but he wouldn't even raise a fist.

Much to my relief, the Lord, my shepherd, led me along the right pathway. In the end I did find a true revolutionary. Unlike Jesus of Nazareth, this revolutionary isn't afraid to fight. He doesn't have great wisdom, and he certainly doesn't claim to be the Messiah. From now on I will courageously prepare for battle and never look back.

Many followers of Jesus of Nazareth tried to justify his failures. Soon after those horrid events, I ran into Mary while at home in Bethany. She tried to convince me, saying, "Do you remember the miracle Jesus performed by raising Lazarus from the dead? Well, he rose from the dead! It happened on the third day."

I laughed at this absurd idea. "We both know the resurrection will take place in the future. Jesus prayed for God's kingdom to come to earth. I watched his kingdom end in shame and humiliation on that cross."

"Jesus came to bring a different kind of kingdom," Mary insisted, "a kingdom of mercy, where the king suffers, dies, and then rises."

Her words stirred resentment in my heart. I scoffed. "You can have your kingdom of mercy where a weak man prays for his enemies. As for me, I will fight for freedom and die if I have to." Mary's face was downcast. She hugged me. "I'll pray for you," she said. As we hugged a flood of memories struck my heart. For a moment I recalled the good times we had following Jesus. But all of that was in vain because he didn't deliver. As Mary walked away, I pitied her. She just couldn't give up on a bad idea. Followers of Jesus of Nazareth won't accept that he failed to establish God's kingdom. The corrupt Romans still rule our land and oppress our people.

I am Deborah, a warrior with a fiery spirit. I urge everyone to listen to my plea. Join me and fight for freedom, like the heroes of Israel. I follow a man who is a true revolutionary, and I pray others will join me. Come and follow the best Jesus I have ever known: Jesus Barabbas.

CHAPTER 2

Shem of Capernaum

MY NAME IS SHEM. I grew up in Capernaum, a quaint fishing town on the north side of the Sea of Galilee. I hope to make a name for myself. In Hebrew, my name actually means "name." Don't get me wrong; Capernaum is a decent town, but I want to be part of something bigger. I'm going to tell you about the rise and fall of Jesus of Nazareth, a man who could never keep a crowd. He could have done amazing things if only he had listened to me.

I am an Israelite. I study the Scriptures and hope to be in the presence of greatness, perhaps even in the company of a great prophet. While I may not be the smartest person in Galilee, I have a passion for leadership. Zebedee, my uncle, gave me work as a fisherman. His sons, James and John, my older cousins, also worked for him, along with several hired hands. Zebedee is a good fisherman; he's just not much of a leader.

After a few years of learning to fish, I was ready to make a name for myself.

"Uncle Zebedee, you need bigger nets," I said one day. "With bigger nets you can catch more fish, and before you know it people in town will be talking about your business."

"These nets," he said pointing at them, "have served me well for years. There's no reason to change."

"Uncle Zebedee," I said, "This is what you need." I revealed an enormous net that I had secretly woven all by myself.

"That will never work," he replied with a chuckle.

"Yes, it will," I insisted. "Take the boat right over there." I pointed to a cluster of fishing boats.

He shrugged. "Go ahead. You'll see."

I cast my giant net deep into the blue waters of the Sea of Galilee as everyone watched. "I'm going to need some help pulling up all these fish!" I said as the weight of my amazing catch nearly tipped the boat over.

"You got lucky, Shem," my uncle said in disbelief.

Meanwhile, James and John jumped out of the boat and dragged my enormous catch ashore. The men in the surrounding boats watched in amazement while those on land gathered to admire my incredible catch. I was the talk of the town. That was the day I knew the Lord had called me to be a leader.

Leadership is like fishing. A good fisherman casts his nets where the fish are while avoiding the spots where the fish are not. Likewise, a good leader attracts and keeps big crowds. While this may sound simple, in practice it is quite difficult. I share my wisdom freely because that's the kind of guy I am. I mentioned my hometown, Capernaum. This was where Jesus of Nazareth lived during most of his teaching days. Before I tell you more about him, let's begin with his cousin, John the Baptist.

People from Jerusalem and all of Judea could not stop talking about this man. I traveled with a crowd to the obscure wilderness of Judea to see what the fuss was all about. As we approached the flowing banks of the famous Jordan River, I noticed this peculiar man who some thought was a prophet. John the Baptist even fashioned himself like one, wearing camel's hair clothing with a leather belt, just like Elijah. Because he wore the clothing of a prophet, many in the crowds were stirred with great interest. Israel hasn't had a prophet in over four hundred years, not since Malachi. John had potential; when he spoke, people listened.

As we approached, his voice boomed like thunder. "Repent!"

That got everyone's attention. John had charisma and a fiery spirit, which won over the masses. I joined a crowd huddled along the shores of the Jordan eager to be baptized. He prayed with me, and soon I was rising from the waters, ready to follow.

John led an extremely strict lifestyle. He spent his days fasting and praying, and the food wasn't great, either. As the novelty of my baptism faded away, I knew he needed my advice. I could help him keep the crowds happy and comfortable. I don't believe that God wants us to be miserable all the time. Several of John's disciples felt the same way but were afraid to speak up.

"Clearly, the Lord has blessed you with the gift of attracting crowds," I told him one day. "I can help you keep them. First, I need to speak a truth that may be difficult to hear. Many of your disciples are not content. If you make them more comfortable, you will gain more followers."

John scratched his long, scraggly beard, deeply pondering my request, and then uttered a single word: "Repent."

His response was beyond frustrating. I was only trying to help. Despite my best efforts to change his mind, John was too stubborn. That was when I decided to look for better options. I wasn't alone. Many disciples joined me.

John would have been more successful had he been more flexible. For example, before I left, he kept blasting the immoral behavior of Herod Antipas. I took him aside for a moment. "I know you mean well by condemning Herod's immorality. He's so dangerous and powerful that he could crush this movement. But you must first gain a bigger crowd before you rock the boat."

Once again John gave the same reply: "Repent." I still don't know if he was speaking to me or Herod. Either way, his obsession with repentance led to his downfall. John attracted a crowd with this message but failed to keep them. Had he taken my advice, his movement would have prospered. Instead, his story ended in tragedy. Herod Antipas ordered John's head to be chopped off and put on a platter. That Herod is a sick man. I don't know how anyone could do such a thing. If John would have listened to me, he would still be alive today.

Fortunately, there was a new prophet in town. His name was Jesus of Nazareth. John admitted he wasn't worthy to carry his sandals. Plus, he was more laid back. Some people even thought he was a drunkard because he hung out with some questionable people. I couldn't argue with the results; crowds were forming.

Jesus came with great power. One day we were fishing when he appeared on the rocky shores of the Sea of Galilee. As he approached Peter and Andrew, I waded in the water to get within earshot.

Jesus looked at them with a crooked smile. "Follow me, and I will make you fish for people."[28]

What a brilliant line! I nearly laughed out loud when I heard these words. Here was a land-loving rabbi using fishing language to relate to these men. I thought, *Finally, a teacher who understands that getting a crowd is like fishing!* I was amazed that such a powerful rabbi would call lowly fishermen to be disciples. Most rabbis only call the best students to follow them. Those who aren't the smartest are left to work the family trade—like fishing. Not Jesus; he called many fishermen to follow him.

A few days later, I was mending the nets with Zebedee, James, John, and some hired hands. Jesus came near the shore, a stone's throw away, and called James and John to follow him. How I wish he had chosen me too! Something big was happening through Jesus; that much was clear.

Growing up in Capernaum, I went to the synagogue and heard the scribes teaching Scripture. They tried their best, but they lacked conviction. The scribes would ramble on about how we should be like Moses and the prophets. While I agreed, they never really inspired people. I tried to help them become better leaders, but they grew defensive. I was only trying to help. I guess a lot of people don't want to put in the work necessary to become a great leader.

But Jesus was different. He said what he meant and meant what he said. He attracted huge crowds. On the next sabbath, I went to our synagogue in Capernaum, knowing it would be no ordinary day. Jesus taught with more passion and energy than I had ever seen. Everyone was captivated. Meanwhile, a man with an evil spirit entered, threatening to ruin the day. Initially, Jesus seemed distracted. Once he made eye contact with the man, he took a deep breath and stepped closer. Then he startled us all with a sudden shout. "Be silent, and come out of him!"[29]

The man fell to the ground and started flopping like a fish out of water as the stunned crowd looked on. Once his convulsions stopped, he slowly opened his eyes and leapt up, shouting, "Alleluia! I'm free! Praise the Lord!" Word spread about Jesus that day. What a day!

Soon massive crowds came out to see him. Jesus was making a name for himself. One day I arrived early to see him teach. He went inside a house while I remained just outside. So many people were crammed in so tightly that I felt like a fish trapped in a net. It was pretty wild. Meanwhile, friends of a paralyzed man did something so incredible I never grow tired of telling this story. Since they had no chance of carrying him to Jesus, they dug a hole in the roof and lowered him inside!

"Son, your sins are forgiven,"[30] Jesus said to the paralyzed man.

That seemed like a weird thing to say. After all, how many sins could a paralyzed man commit anyway? Then Jesus took it to a whole new level.

"I say to you, stand up, take your mat and go to your home."[31]

Sure enough, the once-paralyzed man strutted out of the house with his mat under his arm. The crowd went nuts! "We have never seen anything like this!"[32] many of them exclaimed. As I felt the energy flowing through the rowdy crowd, I knew bigger things were coming soon.

Jesus also created a controversy. The scribes took issue with how he forgave the sins of the paralyzed man. They said only God could do that. While I had never seen a person forgive sins, I had never seen anyone heal with such authority either. Maybe the scribes were right, and maybe they were wrong, but the crowd remained enthusiastic, which was all I needed to know. I prayed I could help Jesus by sharing my wisdom. Between his charisma and my advice, we could make names for ourselves.

A few days later, thousands of people went out to see Jesus. What a sight! He taught for a while, and everything was going well. However, the twelve apostles were in a panic because they were nearly out of food, and the people were hungry. They tried to reason with their rabbi. "Send the crowd away," they said, "so they may go into the surrounding villages and the countryside, to lodge and get provisions; for we are here in a deserted place."[33]

Jesus was calm, almost too calm given the crisis at hand. "You give them something to eat,"[34] he replied.

This reminded me of when the prophet Elijah asked the widow to give him some food before God provided a miracle. The disciples hastily gathered some loaves and fish. Jesus ordered us to sit down, and then he looked toward heaven and prayed. Suddenly, bread and fish were everywhere! There was so much food, enough to feed thousands, not counting the leftovers. People began dancing and singing as they celebrated this great miracle.

"Who is this guy?" one elderly woman asked. "Is he a prophet like Jeremiah or Elijah?"

"He is John the Baptist raised from the dead," a young man confidently asserted.

"Might he be the Messiah?" several more wondered.

He had built a bigger crowd than I had ever seen, and the roars of approval were intoxicating. Israel has waited a long time to be restored. The people sought to honor Jesus by crowning him as king. Finally, he received the admiration of the crowd. When the big moment arrived, I had chills down my spine. This would be comparable to the anointing of King David. Everyone expected a speech about his kingdom, but to my utter shock, he ran away and headed for the hills. To this day, I have no idea what he was thinking. Good leaders give the people what they want. There is no excuse for running away from an adoring crowd. Maybe he wasn't ready. Maybe he was scared. Whatever his excuse, Jesus cast his net in the wrong place. He still had much to learn, and I hoped to help him before it was too late.

Later that day, the strangest thing happened. I watched the twelve get into their boat while Jesus went the other way. When

I arrived at Capernaum, people were talking. Some claimed he walked on water while others said he got into another boat. If he walked on water, only a fool would do such an impressive miracle away from the crowd. Between fleeing his coronation and doing miracles in private, his mistakes were adding up.

I was glad to find Jesus back in Capernaum. Once again, he taught in our synagogue. He used the phrase "I Am," just as God did with Moses. Perhaps he was claiming to be God or like God. Jesus also said, "I am the bread of life."[35] He spoke about the time in the wilderness when God fed the Israelites with manna from heaven. I didn't understand. I think he was comparing himself to that heavenly bread. Then he shocked everyone with the following words: "Those who eat my flesh and drink my blood abide in me, and I in them."[36] The idea of eating his flesh and drinking his blood offended, well, everyone.

"How can this man give us his flesh to eat?"[37] the people asked in horror. Everyone firmly rejected this ridiculous teaching. If Jesus had a trusted advisor, like me, he could have avoided this humiliation. He promised to teach his disciples to fish for people, but he was scaring off all the fish! It didn't take long for the entire crowd to abandon him; even the disciples wanted out. I watched as thousands of people walked away in disappointment. This memory still brings tears to my eyes. Crowds don't lie. I joined them, knowing there is strength in numbers. Earlier, I was jealous of James and John. That evening I felt relief that I could go about my life in peace. My cousins were not so lucky.

Of course, this didn't mean I stopped paying attention to Jesus. He still had potential. While fishing with Zebedee, I explained the many failures of Jesus and how to correct them. Sometimes I talked so much that he said I was scaring away all the fish. I told James and John to ask for more power and influence. Even though I wasn't a disciple, I could still help out. If he took my advice, I would seek to become his advisor.

Eventually, James and John went directly to Jesus. Finally, all of my talking paid off. I heard they got scared and asked their mom to help out, although that could have been a rumor. My cousins asked for permission to sit on either side of him in heaven. Jesus failed to understand this great wisdom; instead, he ranted about discipleship. Worst of all he said, "Whoever wishes to become great among you must be your servant, and whoever wishes to be first among you must be the slave of all."[38] How could he compare greatness to serving as a slave? That was exactly the problem!

A good leader attracts power and influence. Why would he teach his disciples to push these good things away? His harsh language about serving like a slave was enough to scare off plenty of potential followers. Crowds don't want to hear that kind of talk. He should have tried to please his disciples, not destroy their ambition.

Another time, Jesus told potential disciples, "If any want to become my followers, let them deny themselves and take up their cross daily and follow me."[39] Why would he say such an outrageous thing? Everybody knows that a cross is a symbol of death and terror. A more reasonable request would have gained greater appeal. He should have said, "Take up your sword and follow me." Plenty of people want to take up a sword, but nobody wants to take up an instrument of Roman torture!

One time an ideal disciple expressed interest in the ministry. This rich young man was obedient to the commandments and had power and money. His wealth alone could have been used to attract many more disciples. Instead of inviting him to follow, Jesus gave him a nearly impossible command: "Sell all that you own and distribute the money to the poor, and you will have treasure in heaven; then come, follow me."[40]

A good leader would have been more realistic. If Jesus had told him to give 20 or even 30 percent to the poor, the young man probably would have followed. Once again, this rabbi claimed to fish for people, yet another fish swam away!

The Lord has a way of giving people second chances. Despite his many blunders, Jesus still had followers near the end. As Passover neared, enormous crowds gathered in Jerusalem. I was standing with them near the Temple when I heard loud shouts. "Hosanna! Blessed is the one who comes in the name of the Lord!"[41] Many people spontaneously grabbed palm branches and waved them in adoration. Suddenly, Jesus dramatically emerged from the crowd riding on a donkey. This fulfilled what the prophet Zechariah said about the Messiah. Everyone was captivated.

I have to give him credit for regaining the crowd's approval. For hundreds of years, we have prayed for the Messiah to appear to lead God's chosen people. The real question on people's hearts and minds was simple: was he the One? Jesus brilliantly set the stage to win over the crowd in a dramatic fashion. He also cleansed the Temple in protest and silenced his opponents by demonstrating his mastery of Scripture. Finally, he was fishing for people again.

Of course, that didn't mean the religious leaders gave up. They tried hard to win the people over. They gathered at the palace of the high priest, Caiaphas, looking for a way to arrest and kill Jesus. "Not during the festival," they wisely decided, "or there may be a riot among the people."[42] They knew emotions run high during the Passover, so they looked for a way to work with the crowd. If only Jesus had their shrewdness.

Instead, Judas turned Jesus over to the authorities. Peter denied knowing him while all the other disciples fled. It all happened so fast. Jesus eventually admitted to being the Messiah, but it was too late.

The next day was his trial before Pontius Pilate. I waited to see if he had one last miracle to perform, but Jesus hardly said a word. When Pilate offered to release a prisoner, the crowd shouted for Barabbas. He may have been a criminal, but he had a strong following. The people were in such a frenzy that a riot was about to break out. Pilate played the crowd perfectly and eventually released Barabbas. I have never cared for Pilate, but I have to give him credit. He gave the people exactly what they wanted while washing his hands of any responsibility. He sure knew how to handle the crowd.

The soldiers made a crown of thorns, mocking his claim to be a king. They beat him up and led him to the cross. The brutality was jarring to witness. I stuck around to see if he might have one dramatic miracle left. Maybe all that talk about the cross had a larger purpose.

The people let him have it on the cross. Some shook their heads in disbelief while many others laughed at him. "He saved others," one man scoffed, "he cannot save himself. He is the King of Israel; let him come down from the cross now, and we will believe in him."[43] While I know his words were sarcastic, there was some truth in them. This was a final invitation for a miracle. Can you imagine if Jesus had come down from that cross? God's power would have been on full display. The crowd would have believed. I would have believed too.

Instead, I watched a grotesque scene play out before my eyes. Like a fish out of water, he gasped for air and writhed in pain. Then he took a deep breath. "It is finished,"[44] he said. His corpse hung from the cross; it was all over. I had to agree with his final words— Jesus was finished. What a shame! The people left because there was nothing to see. He was not the Messiah.

That is where this terrible story should have ended. Sadly, the death of Jesus opened even more wounds. A little while later, James and John came back home to Capernaum. They looked like they had seen a ghost, but they were shouting with excitement. "Jesus has risen from the dead!"

"Come on, guys," I said, laughing at their words. "I know we fishermen tend to exaggerate. I watched him die on that cross. I heard his painful last words, 'It is finished.' Don't you understand? Finished."

"Listen, I know this sounds crazy," James asserted. "He said this would happen, but we didn't believe him. Come and see for yourself, Shem."

"You know I love you," I replied, feeling pity for my cousins. "Can't you see that Jesus died of stubbornness? I'm afraid you're beginning to sound just like him."

"He knows how to fish for people," John insisted. "Trust me."

"Why should I trust you?" I replied. "You should trust me. After all, I warned John the Baptist about Herod Antipas. He didn't listen to me, and his head ended up on a platter!"

"Shem," James said, "you know that Jesus was different—"

"Exactly," I snapped. "Jesus was superior to John. Look what happened to him. He was tortured to death. Go tell the rest of the twelve that their lives are in danger."

My heart sank as I looked into their eyes. My cousins, along with their mother, were determined to follow Jesus. Before they could leave, Zebedee gave one final plea.

"I have given my life for this family," he said. "Nothing is more important than family. You can be in charge of the fishing business. All that is mine is yours if you'll just stay with me."

James, John, and their mother hugged the poor old man and wiped the tears from his eyes. "Father," James said, "we will always love you, but Jesus called us to fish for people, and that's what we are going to do. Come with us."

"Shem said your lives are in danger. My poor old heart can't handle the thought of you perishing like Jesus did. I don't understand why you'd leave home to follow a dead man."

They wouldn't stop their fanatical speech, and soon left town.

Over the years we received various reports that most of the twelve had been executed. This needless suffering could have been prevented if they had listened to me.

Poor old Zebedee lost his mind. I did my best to support him. I knew better than to mention Jesus in his company. He hated that man so much. I don't blame him when I think of the heartache Jesus brought his way. I tear up as I recall Zebedee's last words to me. "Shem, I won't live until sunset. But the truth is that I have already died. The day that my wife and children left me to follow that dead man's ghost, that was the day that I died."

These days I own the fishing business that my late uncle left me. I still live in Capernaum, and I have made a name for myself. I catch more fish than anyone else on the Sea of Galilee. I'm the talk of the town. If only Jesus had listened to me, his story would not have ended in tragedy, and poor old Zebedee would have been spared his suffering. Some fools still follow Jesus. They willingly take up their cross, which is something nobody should ever do. On the shores of the Sea of Galilee, he promised to teach his disciples to fish for people. He died a failure with no crowd to support him.

Jesus left a terrible legacy of disappointment, heartache, and death. Listen to my words or risk sharing his fate.

CHAPTER 3

Sarah of Nazareth

MY NAME IS SARAH of Nazareth, and I am a Galilean Jew. I have so many stories about Jesus. After all, he was raised here in Nazareth. I will tell you about that terrible day when he enraged the good people of our synagogue. Sadly, he kept teaching shameful nonsense until he was caught, tried, and crucified. Before I get into all of that unpleasantness, let me tell you about myself.

My family has lived in Nazareth for generations. We have a proud Jewish genealogy. I was named after the great biblical figure Sarah, who is known as a mother of nations. My husband, Hezekiah, can build anything with his hands. Together we have four beautiful children and nine grandchildren. We don't have much, but we stick together because we are family.

I spend most of my days preparing meals, praying, and caring for my grandchildren. I may be old, but I'm still going strong. There's nothing more important than faith and family. Some children in Nazareth don't have much family and don't know the Lord. I take these little ones under my wings. People often call me "Mother Hen." While I didn't like that nickname at first, I have grown to appreciate it. After all, a mother hen is both nurturing and fiercely protective of her little ones, just like me.

Every year before we travel to Jerusalem to celebrate Passover, I gather my grandchildren to teach them about the past. As Israelites, the Lord has given us an amazing heritage. I pray my instructions will help them appreciate their history. The best way I can tell the sad story of Jesus of Nazareth is by sharing my most recent "Grandmother Hen talk," as the little ones call them.

I began by leading the children up to one of the many hills in Nazareth. "Gather under this shade tree," I said on that warm sunny day. I had led them to that exact spot for reasons I would later explain. "As the Psalms declare," I began, "'This is the day that the Lord has made; let us rejoice and be glad in it.'[45] I give thanks for the chance to teach you to walk in the ways of the Lord. You all have good Jewish names, and your fathers have given you much instruction in the Scriptures. I don't have many days left, so remember this proverb: 'Train children in the right way, and when old, they will not stray.'[46] What do you suppose this means?"

Little Sarah, whose name my daughter gave her in my honor, spoke up. "I think it means if we learn the right things now, we will make wise choices as adults."

I beamed with pride as she spoke with maturity beyond her years. "Exactly. I have made my life's work the pursuit of obeying Scripture. Believe me, this is not always easy, but the Lord is faithful and rewards those who endure. Now, children, look out over those rolling hills. Most people beyond those hills don't understand our way of life. Suppose an outsider came and asked you about our town. What would you tell them about Nazareth?"

This time, Rueben, my eldest grandson, spoke up. "Nazareth is a Jewish farming village in the region of Galilee. In addition to farming, many of our men work with their hands, especially as stone workers. Outsiders often make fun of our small town, saying things like, 'Can anything good come out of Nazareth?'[47] But they underestimate us. We are God's chosen people. We may be small, but we are mighty."

"Very good, Rueben," I replied. "You are correct that many outsiders don't appreciate our way of life. Why do you think this is the case?"

My second-eldest grandson, Seth, chimed in. I was nervous because he tends to challenge authority. To my surprise, he gave an excellent answer. "The Lord gave us this land. Later, a group of non-Jews, or Gentiles, invaded. Led by Caesar, they oppress our people and plunder countless towns like ours, making us build temples to their false gods. For generations, going back to the prophet Isaiah, this area has been known as 'Galilee of the Gentiles.'"[48]

"Galilee of the Gentiles," I reminded the children. "The Lord gave us this land long ago. There are so many faithful Jews in Galilee. I pray for the day when people start calling this land 'Galilee of the Jews.' Of course, not everyone from Nazareth honors our heritage. Can anyone give me an example?"

Another grandchild, Miriam, gulped nervously. She's a smart girl but painfully shy. "Yes, Grandmother Hen," she said. "People often make fun of us because of, well, you know who. My parents won't let me say his name."

"Go ahead, Miriam. I spoke to your parents. You are allowed to say his name."

"Jesus of Nazareth," Miriam muttered with her head held low. "That's what people call him, at least."

"Hearing that name pierces my heart like a sword, even though years have passed since his death. Most of you were not even born then. Today I will tell you the true story of Jesus of Nazareth."

The children were greatly intrigued. Year after year I taught them about the great heroes of Israel—Moses, Elijah, Jeremiah, David, and more. None of those talks captured their attention as much as a story about that scoundrel, Jesus.

"But first, children, I want to know what you have heard about him. What do your parents or friends say about Jesus?"

"He was crucified," Seth replied. "I heard he thought he was the Messiah, but we all know that isn't true. We tried to stop him, but he escaped."

"Every time my father hears his name," Rueben said, "he turns red and says words that I'm not allowed to repeat. He told me that Jesus insulted our people while praising outsiders."

"Very good, children. Today I will tell you why your father turns red at the sound of his name, and why Jesus was crucified—"

"Grandmother Hen," little Sarah interrupted, "was Jesus always mean? When he was young, what was he like?"

"He was a sweet little boy. He played games just like you do, studied Scripture, and helped his family. I only remember one time when he got into real trouble. One year when Jesus was twelve years old, we had finished celebrating Passover in Jerusalem. A caravan of people from Nazareth headed home, as we continue to do to this day. An entire day into the journey, Mary and Joseph discovered Jesus was missing. I had never seen her so worried. Joseph and Mary ran until a cloud of dust trailed behind them. They searched Jerusalem with haste until they finally found Jesus in the Temple. Mary was equally furious and relieved. 'Child,' she said, 'why have you treated us like this? Look, your father and I have been searching for you in great anxiety.'⁴⁹ Children, until you become parents, you'll never understand the feeling of losing a child, even for a moment. Do you think I would put up with such behavior?"

"No way!" they exclaimed.

"That's right. Worst of all, that boy had the nerve to talk back. He said, 'Why were you searching for me? Did you not know that I must be in my Father's house?'⁵⁰ Nobody knew what he meant. Did he not understand that his father was Joseph? If you ask me, his problems began that day when he disrespected his parents. I think you all know better, right?"

"Yes, Grandmother Hen," the children said in unison.

"Good. As I was saying, for the most part, Jesus was well behaved. Even as a young child, he knew Scripture better than most adults. He always had wise questions for anyone who would listen. He was gifted, but in my experience, gifted children often cause the most trouble for their parents. Isn't that right, Seth?"

The children giggled and Seth smiled with glee, recognizing the truth of my words.

"Other than that one time, was Jesus obedient to his parents?" Miriam asked.

"Absolutely. He worked with his father, Joseph, may his soul rest in peace. As a carpenter, Joseph taught his sons how to work with their hands, which is probably why he and Hezekiah got along so well. They often traveled together to work in nearby towns. One of these cities you all know quite well, Sepphoris. People call it the 'Jewel of Galilee.' But that's not the real story. They forget that poor Jewish laborers from small towns like ours made this city so beautiful. We did most of the work for meager wages, yet nobody outside of Nazareth remembers.

"Back in those days, before any of you were born, there was a major construction project in Sepphoris. Many of the ornate buildings that stand today are the result of the talented men of Nazareth. Grandpa Hezekiah crafted some breathtaking mosaics, including the one honoring Abraham. I know you've all seen that one. He is the greatest craftsman west of the Jordan River! One day his boss did the most detestable thing. He ordered Hezekiah to build mosaics honoring false gods. Can you believe the nerve of this man?"

"Isn't that against the commandments?" Seth asked.

"Exactly," I affirmed. "Grandpa Hezekiah boldly defended his faith, saying, 'Boss, I love working with my hands, but I am an Israelite. I can't build a mosaic honoring false gods. Please let me work on a different project,' he begged.

"His boss was a Gentile who didn't fear God. He merely scoffed. 'You're an Israelite, huh? Don't you know that one of your people ordered all of this work? Herod Antipas gave these orders. If you don't like them, go tell him yourself!' He laughed and laughed. From that day forward, his boss tried to make Hezekiah's life miserable.

"Now children, understand that Herod Antipas was not one of us. He may have been an Israelite in name, but he always served Caesar's interest. Don't get me started on the crushing taxes we paid so Herod could have another palace! Meanwhile, people in Nazareth nearly starved to death. Betraying your people is the most shameful thing I can imagine. If you ask me, Herod was worse than any Gentile. He was a wolf in sheep's clothing. I'm sorry for getting so passionate."

"Grandmother Hen," Miriam said, "how do you stay hopeful?"

"Well, Miriam," I paused to collect my emotions and then continued, "I take comfort in the proverb, 'Grandchildren are the crown of the aged.'[51] I find my hope in you. I also find hope in Scripture, particularly the prophets. For example, Isaiah promised things will change when the Messiah comes. Every night I pray the following words from the prophet: 'The spirit of the Lord is upon me, because the Lord has anointed me; he has sent me to bring good news to the oppressed, to bind up the brokenhearted, to proclaim liberty to the captives, and release to the prisoners; to proclaim the year of the Lord's favor, and the day of vengeance of our God.'[52] These words will be spoken by the Messiah one day. That gives me hope.

"When the Messiah comes, our days of humiliation will be over. The day of vengeance is the best part. Isaiah explains, 'Strangers shall stand and feed your flocks, foreigners shall till your land and dress your vines . . . Because their shame was double, and dishonor was proclaimed as their lot, therefore they shall possess a double portion; everlasting joy shall be theirs.'[53]

"The Lord will humiliate our enemies while putting us in charge. That will be a mighty fine day indeed. Do you understand?"

"I think so," Rueben said. "Our suffering will finally end. Plus, we'll get revenge on our enemies. I can't wait for the Messiah to do this!"

"That's right, Rueben!" I affirmed. "This reminds me of a psalm, 'May those who sow in tears reap with shouts of joy.'[54] The Lord has promised victory. Therefore, we must remain strong until this wonderful day."

"What about Jesus?" little Sarah asked. "What happened when he got older?"

"Most of what you need to know happened on one terrible day," I explained. "He returned to Nazareth when he was thirty years old. We had not seen him in a long while. All I knew were the reports I heard from his mother, Mary. He was spending time with John the Baptist, near the Jordan, before returning home.

"The day began in typical fashion as we gathered at the synagogue. I recognized Jesus immediately. He had a stern and commanding presence, lean muscles, and a longer beard than before. The attendant handed him the scroll of the prophet Isaiah. He slowly unrolled it, paused, and then spoke those beautiful words I pray each night, 'The spirit of the Lord is upon me, because the Lord has anointed me . . .'[55]

"Every single eye was glued on Jesus. There was a stunned silence until finally, a few people spoke up. 'That man has some conviction,' one man said. 'Might this Scripture be fulfilled soon?' another added joyfully. My heart raced at this thought. Nothing would have brought me greater joy.

"Jesus ignited the synagogue. Hope pulled one way, skepticism the other. Despite the tension, he slowly scanned the gathering, which only built the anticipation for his next words. He continued reading from Isaiah. Then he dramatically declared, 'Today this Scripture has been fulfilled in your hearing.'"[56]

"Wait, wait, Grandmother Hen. I'm confused," Rueben interrupted. "What did he mean? Did Jesus seriously think he was the Messiah?"

The other children leaned in close to hear my answer.

"Oh yes, I can still hear the people gasp. He thought the prophet Isaiah wrote those words about him!"

"Did the people believe him or not?" Seth pressed.

"Well, that depends on who you ask," I explained. "I think most people felt like me. They loved the idea of the coming Messiah, but few could imagine God's anointed coming from lowly Nazareth. Then a single question from the crowd perfectly summarized our doubts: 'Is not this Joseph's son?'[57]

"Now children, let's pause and see how well you were paying attention. Did Jesus give us the full story from the prophet Isaiah?"

"No," Miriam answered, "He didn't say anything about getting revenge on our oppressors."

"That's right, Miriam. You're so smart," I said. "He had no harsh words about our enemies, even though we desperately wanted to hear them. Of course, he wasn't done teaching either. Since the people of Nazareth are reasonable and patient, we let him clarify.

"Next, Jesus told two biblical stories. The first was about Elijah and the widow at Zarephath. Can any of you summarize this story? How about you, Rueben?"

"Sure, I will try," he said. "God sent our great Jewish hero Elijah on a mission. He went to Zarephath in the region of Sidon during a famine to meet a widow. Zarephath is a nasty place full of pagan worship. My parents would never let me go there. Then Elijah met the widow and requested food. She refused because she and her son were starving. When the prophet explained how the Lord would provide, she finally gave him the food. Then the Lord miraculously provided enough for them all. Is that right?"

"Yes, excellent," I replied. Then I quizzed them. "Who was the hero in this story?"

"Elijah, of course!" Seth chirped with enthusiasm.

"Yes, but why?"

"Because he trusted in the Lord's instruction and convinced the doubting widow to obey."

"You are paying attention today," I said with great surprise. "Now, children, listen to how Jesus shamefully interpreted this Scripture. He said, 'But the truth is, there were many widows in Israel in the time of Elijah . . . yet Elijah was sent to none of them except to a widow at Zarephath.'⁵⁸ Did you notice how he included a detail not mentioned in Scripture?"

The children stared blankly at me for a moment. "I suppose the Scriptures didn't mention any Jewish widows," Miriam said.

"Exactly," I replied. "Jesus said the Lord could not find a single faithful widow in all of Israel. So, God used a Gentile! Why would he insult his people like that? Any self-respecting teacher of Israel should celebrate our great faith, not ridicule us. Never in my life had I heard anyone insult widows, much less a man who had just claimed to be the Messiah. Sorry, children, I know I get pretty passionate. I just love the Lord so much that it pains me to recount that dreadful day."

I took a deep breath and then continued. "How I wish that was the end of this terrible story. Next, Jesus disrespected his

33

people again, this time recalling the story of Elisha and Naaman. Miriam, do you remember this story?"

"Yes, Grandmother Hen," she said. Then she summarized it. "The Lord sent the great Jewish prophet, Elisha, to a leper named Naaman. He was a commander in the Syrian army, which was a wicked enemy. They kidnapped one of our girls on a raid and made her serve Naaman's wife. Anyway, Naaman got leprosy. He deserved this punishment for the horrible things he had done. The Israelite girl convinced him to seek healing with the help of the prophet Elisha. When Elisha gave instructions to Naaman, he refused. Eventually, the evil Naaman gave in. Sure enough, the Lord miraculously healed his leprosy."

"Thank you, Miriam," I said. "Children, notice how similar these two stories are. Once again, there is a faithful Jew, a reluctant Gentile, and a miracle from the Lord. Now, it pains my heart to remember what happened next. Jesus said, 'There were also many lepers in Israel in the time of the prophet Elisha, and none of them was cleansed except Naaman the Syrian.'[59] Nonsense, I tell you! Jesus had the nerve to criticize his people again. Now, I know most people don't care much for lepers, but those poor people don't need anyone criticizing them. They already suffer enough. What bothers me most is that he praised Naaman. He was an enemy military leader, the worst, yet Jesus thought he was chosen by the Almighty Lord!"

"That's outrageous!" Rueben scoffed in disbelief. "How dare he approve of such a vile person? It's almost as though he liked our enemies, or worse, maybe he loved them."

"Exactly," I replied. "At least when our enemies insult us, we expect those sinners to behave like that. For one of our own people to claim to be the Messiah and then attack our faith—it's beyond words. The first example irritated people, but the second enraged the synagogue. His words betrayed Scripture. He had to be a false prophet.

"Does anyone know what Scripture tells us to do in such a situation?" None of the children answered, so I explained. "Here in Nazareth, we take the commandments seriously. Leviticus instructs us to put such people to death.⁶⁰ The last thing we need is a false teacher polluting the minds of our precious children. That is why I fiercely protect you like a mother hen. "After Jesus spoke, people grew more agitated. Some shook their fists at him. One man yelled, 'You're not the Messiah! You're a liar!' Another shouted, 'Naaman was the worst! You're a traitor!' Then Hezekiah shouted, 'He is a wolf!' 'In sheep's clothing!' the others replied. Within moments the people began joining in a spontaneous call and response, 'He is a wolf . . . in sheep's clothing!' The chants helped the people of Nazareth speak with one voice. The noise was deafening."

"How did Jesus respond? What happened next?" the children asked, eager to hear every detail.

"Calm down. I'm getting there," I said. "Children, I led you to this specific hill today for a reason. This exact spot is where this event happened. Jesus knew he was in trouble. He dashed up this steep, rocky hill beyond that old tree." I pointed uphill, recalling the events as though they had happened yesterday. "The crowd was in hot pursuit. Several threw stones, but none of them managed to strike him. We sought to give him one quick push off the cliff to end it all. As the chants continued, Jesus ran higher and higher until he was near the top. Even the animals were wise enough to scatter. Suddenly, the chants fizzled. 'Where did he go?' Hezekiah asked. 'He was just right there,' others muttered in confusion. 'Does anyone else see him?' another asked in disbelief. Somewhere in the chaos, he slipped away. The plan to hurl Jesus off the cliff failed despite our best efforts to fulfill Scripture."

"Even though he got away," Rueben consoled me, "I'm proud of how our people stayed united."

"Thank you," I replied. "The good people of Nazareth rallied together, refusing to accept his lies. We may be a small town, but we are mighty in faith. Do you understand?"

"Yes," Seth answered. "Jesus thought he was the Messiah. Then, instead of ushering in a future where our Gentile enemies are our servants, he praised them while insulting his own people. This man did not come from God."

"You speak the truth," I said, tearing up. "It's so sad. What breaks my heart is his poor mother. I thought back to when Jesus was a boy. Mary knew he was different. She delighted in hearing him tell her about Scripture passages celebrating the God of Abraham, Isaac, and Jacob. Yet all of this potential was wasted. This once-gifted boy grew up and turned on his people. Poor Mary. The whole family endured such humiliation. I thank the Lord that Joseph didn't live to see this dreadful day!

"If you ask me, he forgot his people. That's the only explanation that makes any sense. I'm telling you this story because I don't want you to turn out like him. Many in Nazareth rejected the entire family after the shameful things that he did. While I find his actions detestable, I felt sympathy for his family. I stayed close to his younger brother, James. He kept track of Jesus and gave me updates from time to time."

"Did he ever learn from his mistakes?" Miriam asked.

"Never." I shook my head in disappointment. "What James told me was worse. Jesus kept repeating the same mistakes. His foolishness reminds me of this proverb: 'Like a dog that returns to its vomit is a fool who reverts to his folly.'"[61]

"Yuk, that's disgusting," the children said. Several of the boys laughed with glee over this amusing proverb.

"That's right, children, his foolishness deserves ridicule." I smiled as their laughter lifted my spirits. "Let me give you another example. One day a Roman centurion had the nerve to ask Jesus to heal his servant. This was a great opportunity for him to speak out against our oppressors. Instead, he granted the centurion's wish, and the centurion believed his words. Jesus said, 'I tell you, not even in Israel have I found such faith.'[62] Did you catch the shameful thing he said?"

Rueben stared in disbelief. "Did Jesus believe a dreadful Gentile soldier had more faith than any Israelite? That's an insult to every man, woman, and child in Nazareth. No wonder so many people hated him!"

"It's sad but true," I said. "Jesus never grew tired of celebrating the most despicable people. A teacher of Israel should speak for us, defend us, and remind everyone that we are the light of the world. We are God's chosen people, after all. Did you know that he even praised prostitutes and tax collectors? Your parents may be upset with me for teaching you about such shameful topics, but you deserve to know the ugly truth. As it is written in Proverbs, 'To keep company with prostitutes is to squander one's substance.'[63] I don't know how he could live with such filth, but it got even worse. Jesus said those deplorable prostitutes have a higher place in God's kingdom than religious leaders! I realize what I am saying sounds unbelievable, shocking, or even made up, but I'm telling you the truth.

"Jesus even told a story celebrating the worst kind of person. Here in Nazareth, we don't even say their names, except when ridiculing them at the end of a joke! Does anyone know who I'm talking about?"

"The S . . . S . . . Samaritans?" Seth stuttered.

"Exactly," I answered. "Let me explain the history, which is a complicated one. Over seven hundred years ago, the brutish Assyrians conquered Israel and took many of our people into captivity. It was horrible. Those invaders resettled our land and brought with them pagan idols. At this point, the people had a choice. Some chose to worship idols alongside the God of Israel. The people who did that were no longer Jews but Samaritans. Those blasphemers dishonored God, but that's not all. They had the nerve to marry those awful Gentiles.

"Meanwhile, our people stayed faithful, even though we were conquered by the Babylonians and carried into captivity. After hundreds of years of suffering, we were finally allowed to return to rebuild Jerusalem. Do you know who opposed our efforts?"

"Those nasty Samaritans, of course!" Sarah exclaimed.

"That's right," I assured the children. "Those people dishonor the Lord's name. I'm glad they worship on Mount Gerizim instead of Jerusalem. They don't deserve to be that close to the Lord. That's why everyone here in Nazareth gladly travels around Samaria and never speaks to those people.

"After all of this painful history, Jesus told a story where the hero was a Samaritan," I said in disbelief. "Everybody knows a person cannot be good *and* a Samaritan. A good Samaritan? There's no such thing. If he likes those people so much, he should have joined them. I bet he would have fit right in!"

"Grandmother Hen," Miriam inquired, "did his family see the warning signs?"

"Yes, Miriam," I said. "James told me something that I still find hard to believe. He said Jesus once traveled to Samaria. The story goes that he talked openly with a Samaritan woman. He stayed with those accursed people for a couple of days. If any of those rumors are true, that's all you need to know about him. Jesus was a traitor and a lover of Samaritans!"

"Wait, wait, Grandmother Hen," Seth interrupted. "Do you expect us to believe all of this? How can a man praise a pagan widow, an enemy military leader, a Roman centurion, tax collectors, prostitutes, and even Samaritans? Your story is too outrageous for me to believe."

I knew it was only a matter of time before Seth would disrespect me. That child can be so frustrating. Fortunately, I was ready, "You are foolish to doubt me. Go ahead, I challenge you to find any follower of Jesus. They will confirm the things I have said today. Beware though because they will try to make his shameful teachings appear noble. That is why I am telling you the truth today. While Jesus may have grown up in Nazareth, he was not one of us at all.

"A moment ago, Miriam asked me about his family. Let me give you another example." As I spoke, Seth hung his head in shame, knowing he was defeated.

"Several months before that horrible day in the synagogue, I was drawing water and chatting with Mary. Her cheeks were pale, and she had a worried look that only a mother can recognize. 'Jesus is doing amazing things,' Mary explained. 'Miracles, I'm told. Yet others are saying that my dear son has gone out of his mind.' Tears flowed down her cheeks as she continued. 'Our family mustered up the courage to save him from himself. We found him and sent word, but he didn't even greet us. Instead, my son looked into the eyes of his disciples and said, 'Here are my mother and my brothers! Whoever does the will of God is my brother and sister and mother.'⁶⁴ Mary burst into tears as I hugged her.

"Poor Mary, he broke her heart. His dear mother gave him life, yet Jesus shamed his flesh and blood. His true family was a group of fishermen, tax collectors, and prostitutes. I don't know how any mother could recover from such an insult."

"Me neither!" several of the kids yelled, with growing agitation.

"Fear not," I encouraged them. "This story has a happy ending. Eventually, enough people caught onto his lies. People in Jerusalem rallied together and gave him justice. He received a trial, was found guilty, and crucified. Crucifixion is terrible. The Romans use this agonizing form of torture to humiliate us. That's why we had the right idea in Nazareth. If we had pushed Jesus off that cliff, his suffering would have ended quickly. Plus, his filthy lies would not have spread to so many innocent ears.

"Many people from Nazareth were in the crowd that day. We remembered his insults and his love of our enemies. We gladly cheered for Barabbas to be released instead. I don't like any of this unpleasantness. I wish it would all go away."

"Did you feel safer once Jesus was gone?" little Sarah asked.

"Absolutely," I assured her. "I felt such relief. Good parents in Nazareth continued to teach Scripture the right way, without enduring shameful attacks on God's chosen people. I always remind little ones that the greatest faith is always found within Israel, never beyond."

"What happened to Mary and James?" Rueben asked.

"That's a sad story," I said. "After Jesus was crucified and buried, his mother was never the same. The grief was too much for her. After all, what mother could accept the death of her son? Instead of dealing with reality, she convinced herself that her son had risen from the dead. Even James believed this nonsense. I tried to reason with them, but it was like arguing with a mule. Those foolish Jesus followers will believe anything! They continue to grow in numbers, like weeds that need to be uprooted. I am so ashamed that people still associate Jesus with Nazareth. Before him we were a small, insignificant town, but he made us a total laughingstock."

"Grandmother Hen," Miriam said, "what can we do about his followers? They are convinced he was the Messiah."

"Dear children, that is why I am teaching you this history lesson today. You should take pride in Nazareth. Followers of Jesus don't honor our people. Most of them don't even understand why we ran him out of town in the first place. I witnessed his shameful love for our enemies and his rebukes of faithful Israelites. The truth is the good people of Nazareth defended our honor that day in the synagogue. The world needs more people like us. Children, you must stand strong and fight to stop the followers of Jesus once and for all."

CHAPTER 4

Maximus Gallus

MY NAME IS MAXIMUS Gallus, but people call me Max. I'm here to tell you about a disobedient troublemaker. He looted, encouraged violence, and doomed many with his contempt for law and order. Although he was a miracle worker, he represented everything wrong with the world. Fortunately, Jesus of Nazareth was crucified for his crimes.

I'm a proud Roman citizen, a soldier, and a family man. I have a beautiful wife and eight children. My dream is to move up the ranks to become a centurion. My brothers, my father, and even my grandfather all served Rome as soldiers. My grandfather and oldest brother paid the ultimate price. I offer my service to honor their legacy. Too many people have already forgotten the great sacrifices our soldiers have made. I would die for Lord Caesar in a heartbeat.

My fellow soldiers respect me because I care more about law and order than anyone. For me, this is personal. My oldest brother, Cato, was an incredible centurion. Many years ago, he was doing security in Jerusalem during Passover. This is a holiday when Jews celebrate how their God allegedly freed them from slavery in Egypt. Things are so much better these days. They are so lucky to live under Lord Caesar, yet some of them are never satisfied. A report came to Cato that a Jewish rabble-rouser was claiming to be a king. This so-called "king" started with a protest, which quickly turned into a riot, as they usually do. Those people make me so angry. Cato quickly ordered many of those seditious rebels to be crucified. Then a gutless Jewish thug snuck up and stabbed my brother in the stomach, then slipped away into the crowd after murdering my hero. I honor Cato every time I catch some lawless rebel or violent thug.

My story can't be told apart from my centurion, Decimus. I still remember the day I met him. I was standing in formation with the other soldiers, waiting to meet our leader. Soon a giant of a man trudged toward us. He wore the typical armor with a silver helmet, topped with red feathers. He was barrel-chested with curly black hair and a full beard. As he approached, his intensity struck fear into our hearts. He swept his beady eyes back and forth, demanding our complete attention.

"I am Decimus," he said, his voice rumbling like thunder. "I am your centurion. You are under my authority. You will do exactly as I say."

Decimus stared down a soldier. "Fetch me a cup of water," he demanded. The poor man looked confused for a moment and then sprinted to find a cup. Several soldiers laughed, but that stopped the moment Decimus glared at them.

Next, he strutted in my direction. My knees nearly buckled in fear. He was so close that I could feel his breath on my cheek as he sized me up. "Soldier, what is your name?"

"My name is Maximus Gallus, sir, but you can call me Max."

"Is that right?" Decimus said, laughing. "Max, since that's what I can call you, let me be clear. I can call you any name I wish. A soldier should know why he fights. Tell them about Lord Caesar and our history. Don't spare any details. You can go all the way back to Julius Caesar."

"The Roman Empire . . ." I stuttered before reciting my deepest convictions. "The Roman Empire is the greatest civilization in the history of the world. We honor our leaders with the name Caesar, recalling the great Julius Caesar. He knew he was likely to be betrayed, so he chose his great-nephew Octavian to be his heir."

Meanwhile, the other soldier returned with a cup of water. Decimus took a sip as I nervously continued.

"Rome was plagued by constant civil wars until Octavian defeated Cleopatra and Anthony at the Battle of Actium. His victory did so much for Rome. Octavian is better known as Caesar Augustus. He ruled when I was born and will always be remembered as one of the greatest leaders ever."

"Max, since I can call you Max," Decimus said, "I can tell you come from a family of soldiers. Now tell us what Caesar Augustus did for us."

"Caesar Augustus . . ." My mind raced to recall every detail. "Caesar Augustus restored the Senate and brought peace to the earth. As the fruits of peace, we began to enjoy great prosperity. Caesar expanded trade, built roads, completed impressive building projects, and most importantly, used the military to secure law and order. Soldiers like us helped with these efforts. Caesar's leadership took Rome from a republic to an empire. That's why we should all be proud to work for the greatest civilization in history."

"Max, in all my years serving under Lord Caesar . . ." He paused and gulped his water while I prepared for the worst. "I have never heard a better answer. Keep it up, and you may be a centurion one day." Once Decimus turned away from me, I grinned at the thought of my dream coming true.

"Now, soldiers," Decimus continued, "let's see if the rest of you know anything. I will start with some easy questions. Who is the Son of God?"

"Caesar!" we all shouted in unison.

"Caesar is . . ."

"Lord!" we affirmed.

Decimus suddenly pounced on another soldier. "What is Advent?"

"Advent is when we gather to honor Caesar's greatness!"

"And what else can you tell me about Caesar?"

"Caesar is our Lord. He's the savior of the world," the nervous soldier recited. "He has brought peace to the earth. Everything in the world belongs to Caesar."

"OK," Decimus affirmed. "This soldier knows a few titles of Caesar, at least the ones engraved on the coins in our pockets. Now line up and march toward that cliff!"

Immediately, we lined up in formation and started marching. Up ahead, I saw the edge of a cliff fast approaching. We continued to march nervously until we were steps away from the edge.

"March, soldiers, march!" Decimus demanded.

The lead soldier was one step away from inevitable death. Nevertheless, he lifted his foot over the edge. Suddenly, Decimus yelled for us to stop.

However, the poor soldier was starting to fall over the cliff. He flailed his arms to regain his balance. As he began to fall, Decimus snatched him with a single hand. He held the terrified soldier the way a child holds a toy while his body dangled over the cliff.

"If I tell you to march over the edge, that is what you will do," Decimus said. "You will die for Caesar if you must." Then he swung the soldier around and set him safely onto the dusty ground before sending us away.

That glorious day inspired me. Seeing the strength of Decimus on display gave me hope that I could become a strong soldier like him one day. From then on, I fought bravely and devoted myself to Caesar with gusto.

One day after a particularly brutal battle, Decimus ordered me to come to him. "Max, you are quickly earning my respect. I want you to take a few days off to relax. I need you to be at full strength for our next battle. Go."

I decided to travel to the Sea of Galilee. Upon my arrival, I took in the glorious scenery. The rocky terrain, the blue water, and the blowing wind were all so peaceful that I drifted off to sleep. I was awakened by the noise of a gathering crowd. I looked on top of the rocky hills above to see what all the fuss was about.

"What's going on here?" I asked a stranger next to me.

"Jesus of Nazareth is about to speak," the man said with glee.

"Who's that?"

"He is a miracle worker and . . ." His voice trailed off as a certain man climbed upon a rock, so we could all see him. He sat down and began teaching.

"Blessed are the poor in spirit," he said, "for theirs is the kingdom of heaven."[65]

Those words made me cringe. "The kingdom of heaven," I mumbled. "Everybody knows that Caesar is the only true king." But that man wasn't finished yet.

"Pray then in this way," he instructed. "Our Father in heaven, hallowed be your name. Your kingdom come. Your will be done, on earth as it is in heaven."[66]

This man talking about bringing his kingdom was so offensive to Lord Caesar, whose kingdom is so great. I even heard somebody suggest this man might be the "Son of God." I had to look down at my sandals to hide my disgust at the way Caesar's titles were being applied to this man.

As Jesus stirred up the crowds, talking about his "kingdom," I was reminded of the day Cato was shamefully attacked. These rabble-rousers seem to come and go with the seasons, promising the world or heaven, but none of them deliver. Instead, all they bring are protests, looting, and riots. Despite all this, the crowds loved Jesus. The worst part came next when he flagrantly attacked law and order.

There's a law that a Roman soldier can order a person to carry an object, such as a soldier's bag or a cross, no more than one mile. Once a fellow soldier got into a scuffle with a man who refused to carry his bag. Such an infraction deserves swift punishment. The soldier grew so angry that he forced the man to carry his bag two miles. While I understand his frustration, not even a soldier is allowed to do this. Decimus exploded in anger. He grabbed his neck and lifted the soldier in the air with one hand. "One mile," he said. "That is the law. If any of you allow somebody to go a step past one mile, I will have you flogged, fined, or worse. Now cut this man's food rations for a month, and get him out of my sight." He tossed the soldier to the ground and stormed off.

Next, Jesus looked at the crowd with a smirk on his face. "If anyone forces you to go one mile, go also the second mile."[67]

Let me be very clear, this is a blatant violation of our great Roman law. Yet the crowd grew excited about his disobedient teaching. My brother died because of people like Jesus of Nazareth, so I was fuming in anger as the crowds departed.

"He is teaching people to rebel against the commandments," one man claiming to be a Pharisee said angrily to his friends. "He breaks our laws, such as healing on the sabbath."

"If he can't follow the laws of Moses, imagine the trouble he will bring upon us when he breaks Roman laws," his friend replied.

I couldn't have said it better myself. Finally, some reasonable voices amongst those foolish sheep.

Several months passed before Decimus gave me a new set of orders. "Max, your merit has earned you the privilege of watching my beloved servant. The poor guy is sick and nearing death. Treat him like your own son. There is a miracle worker who I believe can heal him. I'm going to Capernaum now to meet with Jesus of Nazareth."

My skin crawled at the mention of his name. Noticing my reaction, Decimus gave me a curious look. "Speak."

"Decimus, it is my honor to serve you. May I report what I have learned about this man?"

He nodded forcefully. "Quickly, soldier."

"This man is no friend of Caesar," I said. "A few months ago, I saw him with my own eyes. He spoke about his kingdom, so he thinks he's a king. Worst of all, he has no respect for law and order. For example, he told people if they are forced to go one mile, to go the second mile too. He may even be leading a rebellion."

"I see," Decimus said, his eyes narrowing with suspicion as he pondered my words. "My orders remain the same. I will take the chance if he can heal my servant."

I watched the servant while Decimus traveled to Capernaum and found Jesus. Later, Decimus explained every detail to me. He approached the teacher and said, "Lord, my servant is lying at home paralyzed, in terrible distress."[68]

"I will come and cure him,"[69] Jesus replied.

"Lord, I am not worthy to have you come under my roof," Decimus said, "but only speak the word, and my servant will be healed. For I also am a man under authority, with soldiers under me; and I say to one, 'Go,' and he goes, and to another, 'Come,' and he comes, and to my slave, 'Do this,' and the slave does it."[70]

Jesus was amazed at his words. "Truly I tell you, in no one in Israel have I found such faith."[71] He was right to be impressed with Decimus, a man who knows what obedience is all about.

As these events were unfolding, I was watching the sick servant. He would scream in agony every few minutes, though his feeble body remained almost motionless. Suddenly, I heard a loud shout, "I'm healed!" I turned around and saw that this man had sprung to his feet, leaping around like a lamb.

"Praise Caesar! It's a miracle," I said, assuming that Caesar or one of the gods had done this.

Later that day I heard Decimus shouting from a distance. "It's a miracle! It's a miracle! Jesus healed my servant."

"Are you sure Jesus did this and not Caesar?"

"Yes, Max," Decimus explained with uncharacteristic tenderness. "Jesus was incredible. I have never met anyone like him."

As he told me every last detail, I grew uneasy with his report. After all, he was praising a lawless rebel who represented everything wrong with the world today.

"I'm happy your servant has been healed," I affirmed with a tense smile. My life is based on order. I respect my centurion and most of all Lord Caesar. How could Decimus praise Jesus and Caesar with the same lips?

Nearly every week after that, Decimus would take me aside and say, "Jesus did it again. He healed another sick person!"

"Very nice," I would reply, biting my tongue. I could never tell him my true thoughts. He was being seduced by this lawless teacher, all because of a few miracles.

"Jesus turned water into wine and walked on water," he told me another time. Those terrible reports never stopped.

"Good," I muttered. "I'm glad." While my lips affirmed his words, my heart knew better. I feared Jesus might destroy my centurion's great faith in Caesar. How could Decimus admire this lawless peasant?

Several months later, Decimus ordered me to go to Jerusalem for the Passover. As I watched the enormous crowds pour into the city, I thought of my late brother, Cato. His murderer could be somewhere in that crowd. Our great governor, Pontius Pilate, does a glorious thing to keep security and honor Caesar. He organizes an incredible parade, celebrating Roman power and strength with a march into Jerusalem. I love how we soldiers march together, some riding on mighty war horses. The sound of drumbeats fills the city so that everyone can experience the power and glory of Caesar. We have a slogan, "Peace through victory." Peace is kept through our military while potential troublemakers are put on notice.

Soon I saw a commotion near the Mount of Olives. I looked into the distance and saw that Jesus was holding a parade of his own. Instead of mighty war horses, he rode on a feeble donkey. Instead of spears and drums, his followers waved palm branches. People chanted for him as if he were an actual king. I pointed this out to a fellow soldier, and we had a good laugh at their pathetic parade. There was no power, no order, and no respect. I would like to see them challenge Caesar with donkeys and palm branches! What a joke!

The crowd was excited, but crowds are fickle. One day they love you, the next day they turn on you. Whatever that whole parade was about, it was insignificant compared to Pilate's parade. As Jesus entered Jerusalem, I made sure to keep an informant nearby to pass on reports about this troublemaker. We have guards in the Temple area to keep order because there are often plenty of protestors.

Of course, not all Jews hold our great laws in contempt. The finest group of Jews I know are called the Sadducees. They collaborate with us by informing us about potential Jewish troublemakers. The high priest is always sympathetic to our cause—we make sure of that! If only more Jews were like the Sadducees. Those people understand Caesar's greatness.

Next, I received a report that Jesus appeared at the Temple with a whip! He looted the place, flipping over tables while animals ran wild. That filthy peasant even poured out the money changers' coins. It was chaos! The money changers do an important service by receiving offerings from the people and keeping the Temple running smoothly. I consider myself a patient man, but his aggressive looting made me angry. He should have been crucified right then and there, if you ask me.

Meanwhile, Jesus continued to stir the pot. He was asked a simple question, "Is it lawful to pay taxes to Caesar, or not?"[72] Now, if he said not to pay taxes to Caesar, he would immediately be arrested for treason. Instead, he said, "Give to Caesar the things that are Caesar's, and to God the things that are God's."[73] Anyone in Rome can tell you that everything in the world belongs to Caesar. Period. Nobody should ever question this obvious truth. Jesus believed some things in this world don't belong to Caesar. Give me a break!

Eventually, one of his followers came to his senses. His name was Judas Iscariot, and his dedication to law and order are worthy of praise. Led by him, a detachment of soldiers and some religious leaders went out to arrest Jesus.

When they arrived, one of his followers pulled out a sword and cut off the ear of the high priest's slave. Unbelievable! That poor man was just doing his job before he was outrageously attacked.

That violent thug was named Simon Peter. This was no casual follower; he was one of the leaders! Who led him to believe he could stoke violence and disobey authority? Jesus, of course. I learned from Judas that his teacher shamefully taught, "Do not think that I have come to bring peace to the earth; I have not come to bring peace but a sword."[74] That's the kind of violent rebellion Jesus tried to stir up. The only one of them with any sense of decency was Judas Iscariot.

Caiaphas, the high priest, listened patiently as the people sought to convince him to put an end to this unstable character.

Some people correctly feared that Jesus might set off a backlash from Rome. "It is better for you to have one man die for the people than to have the whole nation destroyed,"[75] Caiaphas wisely explained.

I am so grateful for men of principle like Caiaphas who can calm the fears of many with their sage advice. His actions saved countless lives. I wish there were more men like him in this world. Few people will ever know how his wisdom preserved the safety of the people in Jerusalem against thugs like Jesus.

Once Jesus was arrested, crucifixion was inevitable. I remember my first crucifixion. I nearly threw up my lunch. I know many people don't have the stomach to do what I do. Not everybody can be a soldier. I have crucified some disgusting people including treasonous rebels, rioters, looters, and other lawbreakers. Basically, people like Jesus. We crucify in plain sight, so everybody knows not to mess with Caesar.

Suppose I'm wrong. What if this peasant was some kind of king? If that were the case, think about his kingdom. Jesus said before the great Pontius Pilate that his followers wouldn't even fight to save him. What kind of king has followers who won't fight? No king whose name should be remembered in history.

Pilate wisely discerned this threat and gave orders for crucifixion. Several soldiers decided to honor this "king" by putting a crown of thorns on his head. They bowed down and hailed him, and everyone had a good laugh at this "King of the Jews." They even put this title on his cross, so those who passed by could see his "throne."

Decimus claimed Jesus could do miracles. I watched him closely. Jesus was so weak, even struggling to carry his own cross. A soldier grabbed a man named Simon of Cyrene to help him carry the cross to Golgotha. Simon respected law and order. He's a good example of following our great laws. I find it ironic that Jesus was helped by the same law that he taught his followers to break.

If that wasn't bad enough, he had sympathy for a fellow who was being crucified next to him. That man was a troublemaker who fought against the Roman Empire. How did Jesus talk to this lawless criminal? He welcomed him with open arms to join him in paradise! Even on the cross, this man was so deluded that he still believed he was a king. Some people never learn.

Jesus of Nazareth wasted his life. He talked about a make-believe kingdom where his crown was of thorns, and he ruled by hanging on a cross. No wonder so many of his followers abandoned him. Yet after he took his final breath, a centurion said, "Truly this man was God's Son!"[76]

How could yet another centurion be so wrong? By charisma this peasant miracle worker had corrupted too many decent soldiers.

A few days later, Decimus summoned me. "Max, have you heard the news about Jesus of Nazareth?"

"Yes, Decimus," I replied with enthusiasm. "I heard all about his looting of the Temple and the way that thug Simon Peter cut off the ear of a good soldier. Fortunately, Pilate had Jesus crucified before a riot broke out over this man with contempt for law and order."

"Max," Decimus said, "here's what I know. Not only did he heal my servant and do many other mighty deeds, he saved the best for last. Jesus rose from the dead!"

"Is that right?" I replied, biting my tongue. "Well, I'm glad to hear it." I lied to my superior. I had no choice. I had already received reports that some of his brainwashed followers were causing more trouble. Of course, many of his followers doubted Jesus rose from the dead. I had to shut my mouth and bury the truth, as painful as it was. If Decimus hadn't been my centurion, I would have told him the error of his ways. Instead, I quietly lost respect for my once-great leader.

Years have passed since Jesus was crucified. I am now living my dream as a centurion. Decimus died in battle a few years ago. I know exactly why. He grew soft after meeting Jesus. While I model my leadership after Decimus in many ways, there is one major exception. He did not know the same Jesus that I knew. I give thanks to Lord Caesar that those days are finally over.

As long as people continue to follow in the footsteps of people like that dangerous criminal from Nazareth, my work will not be complete. I will stand up against all forces of chaos and lawlessness. My grandfather and Cato paid the ultimate price for Caesar. That is why I serve. Above all, I give thanks to the one who brings peace on earth, whose name is above all names. He is the Son of God and the Savior of the world. Caesar is Lord! May the great name of Caesar be praised forever and ever!

CHAPTER 5

Aaron of Arimathea

MY NAME IS AARON of Arimathea. I am here to warn you about a false teacher named Jesus of Nazareth who twists the Scriptures as he pleases. He criticizes the most righteous among us while praising notorious sinners. I have witnessed such insults with my own eyes.

Arimathea is a small Jewish town that I call home. It's located in the hill country of Judea, northwest of Jerusalem. My parents struggled throughout my childhood. My father was a day laborer, with a vicious temper. When he didn't have enough work, he drank, often settling arguments with his fists. He abandoned our family when I was only a boy.

I grew angry with the world and soon rebelled by hanging out with sinners. I bullied so many kids, more than I can remember. Once I beat a young man so badly that I nearly killed him. The image of his bloody face stuck in my mind and led me to search my heart. I knew I needed to change my ways, or I would end up just like my father.

In the synagogue on the next sabbath, a Pharisee read from Proverbs. "Those who keep the law are wise children, but companions of gluttons shame their parents."[77] I was convicted of my many sins. I knew my time with the "companions of gluttons" had to end, and I needed to trust in the guidance of Scripture. With fear and trembling, I approached the holy Pharisee. Bursting into tears,

I said, "I want to change. I want a pure heart and there is nobody more righteous than a Pharisee. Will you help me?"

I felt a strong hand gently touch my shoulder as I sobbed. The distinguished Pharisee stroked his long white beard and looked intently into my eyes. "Yes, my son," he said. "Yes."

The man's name was Joseph of Arimathea. He was a wealthy, respected man who served on the council, the Sanhedrin, a group of righteous leaders who make decisions about important matters. He had a quiet dignity about him.

Joseph wasted no time before he began instructing me. "Dear Aaron, I will feed you with Scripture like an ox. Make friends with Abraham, Moses, and the prophets. Study the law, pray, and let the Lord guide you."

"Absolutely," I affirmed with vigor.

For much of the next year, I immersed myself in Scripture, and my heart grew in faith. One particular passage inspired me. After Moses died, the Lord led Joshua to inherit the Promised Land, offering these words: "Only be strong and very courageous, being careful to act in accordance with all the law that my servant Moses commanded you; do not turn from it to the right hand or to the left, so that you may be successful wherever you go."[78]

I memorized these holy words and recited them daily. I would follow all the law, never turning from it, and meditating on it day and night. Some people these days only honor some of the laws of Moses, picking and choosing the most important ones. I vowed to always follow the Scriptures strictly. I still sensed the Lord calling me to bigger things.

"Joseph," I said, after mustering the courage to make my request, "I would like to be a Pharisee, like you."

"Would you like to be a Pharisee or be like me?" Joseph quipped. He often answered a question with another question. "Remember, the Lord calls you to be you—not me. As for being a Pharisee, that is another matter indeed."

"Yes, I want to be a Pharisee," I said firmly. "I want to be holy. I have turned away from the sinners who led me astray. Nobody follows the Scriptures with more zeal than the Pharisees. I'll be safe if I surround myself with such people."

"Dear Aaron, I'm an old man now, and I've seen many young men like you come and go. They all start like you, with great passion for the Lord. People admire them and greet them in the marketplace. For some Pharisees, the pressure to appear holy becomes more important than actually being holy. Inevitably, this path leads to hypocrisy. I don't want that for you. Be careful. Focus upon your heart rather than outer appearances. Do this and you will be an excellent Pharisee."

"Joseph," I said with confusion, "I thought you would be more excited."

"I want what's best for you," he affirmed, to my relief. "That is why you must pray about this choice."

"I will," I promised.

Some time passed before I made a decision that will forever define me. I became a Pharisee, thanks to Joseph's guidance and God's grace.

"As a Pharisee," Joseph said with pride, "you are now a shepherd to the sheep of Israel. You are like a son to me."

"Thank you, Joseph," I said as I hugged him. "You are the father I never had."

What a blessing to worship a God who gives people second chances. In my case, God gave me a second father.

Life as a Pharisee was fantastic. I felt free from my past, and for the first time in my life, I felt truly safe. Yet my treasured sense of security was soon threatened by a stranger named Jesus of Nazareth.

One afternoon another Pharisee came to town. His name was Simon. He was well-dressed, articulate, and very formal. "Joseph, good to see you," he said. "It's been a while. Who is this young man?"

"Greetings, Simon. I'm Aaron, and I recently became a Pharisee."

"Congratulations!" Simon exclaimed. "The Lord certainly needs more righteous leaders like you."

"I'm excited to see you. It has been far too long," Joseph said with a look of surprise. "To honor this visit, my family will prepare a feast of bread, fish, and wine for us to enjoy tonight. Let's gather firewood, then we will talk over dinner."

After gathering the firewood, we washed our hands and said several prayers, which are important traditions that Pharisees keep. Joseph was an incredible host. He greeted us with a kiss and provided water to wash our dusty feet and oil to anoint our heads. Even as a child, I remember my family offering a kiss, water, and oil as symbols of hospitality to our guests. Joseph shared love and grace and made me feel like the most important person in the world. Then we enjoyed dinner while watching the sunset together. Soon the fire replaced the sun as our source of warmth, and our conversation began.

"The Sanhedrin has been talking about a man," Joseph said with seriousness. "There are many reports about him, but they all contradict each other. Some claim he is a prophet while others say he has a demon. His name is Jesus of Nazareth."

"I'm so glad you mentioned him," Simon replied. "I have already begun pursuing this task. I fear we are in great danger. Jesus calls himself the 'Good Shepherd,' as if he believes he is more of a shepherd than us. He could be dangerous."

"Dangerous?" I asked in fear.

"Oh yes, dangerous," Simon insisted. "Listen to these words, 'Now you Pharisees clean the outside of the cup and of the dish, but inside you are full of greed and wickedness. You fools! Did not the one who made the outside make the inside also?'[79] That's what Jesus said. This is an outrageous attack on us. If we violate our purity laws, we dishonor the Lord."

Simon's words made me uneasy. Joseph stared quietly at the fire, poking the embers with a stick. After a few moments of silence, he muttered a question. "Was he wrong?"

"What did you say?" Simon raised his voice with righteous anger. "Are you seriously defending this man who insults us?"

"I'm not defending him," Joseph replied. "I'm merely asking if he's wrong. Do Pharisees care more about outer appearances than the condition of the heart? You have to admit, this is a worthy question to ponder."

"I'm confused," I said. "I thought Pharisees agreed on almost everything."

"Oh, Aaron," Simon said with endearment, "you still have a lot to learn. I'm trying to protect us from danger. Jesus has said many horrible things about us. For example, 'You blind guides! You strain out a gnat but swallow a camel! . . . Woe to you, scribes and Pharisees, hypocrites! For you are like whitewashed tombs, which on the outside look beautiful, but inside they are full of the bones of the dead and of all kinds of filth.'[80] Did you hear all of that? There's plenty more where that came from. That teacher delights in insulting us and questioning our holiness, as though we were a bunch of sinners."

"Well, aren't we still sinners?" Joseph pressed. "The Psalms declare, 'There is no one who does good.'[81] I fear too many Pharisees ignore the sin that dwells deep within our hearts."

"Joseph, you're lecturing us," Simon complained. "I know we are all sinners. Yet, we are righteous examples to the people. Look around; we are living in a sinful era much like the times of Noah. We have tax collectors exploiting us, the Temple serving Caesar's interests, and horrible sinners refusing to repent. If things get much worse, I fear we may return to exile. Pharisees strive to defend everything holy. We help the people interpret Scripture. We should be praised for our efforts, not insulted."

Simon sure had a way with words. As he spoke, I felt a surge of righteous anger arise within my heart. I admired his zealous devotion.

"Simon and Aaron," Joseph instructed. "Please go find Jesus, and bring me a full report about his teachings. I must go to the Sanhedrin. We will meet again right around this fire." We finished our fish and our wine and put out the fire. There was work to be done, and it started at sunrise.

The next morning as the roosters crowed, Joseph was already gone. As Simon loaded his donkey with supplies, he explained the plan. "We will travel to my house and invite Jesus over for dinner.

I will tell many Pharisees to join us. That way we can observe him with our own eyes."

"Thank you, Simon," I said.

Our journey began along a narrow dusty road. After a few hours, we caught up with a fellow traveler. He was a burly man with long, wild brown hair. His voice sounded like a scream. "The name is Bartimaeus, son of Timaeus," he said. "I'm from Jericho. Whom do I have the pleasure of meeting?"

"Greetings," Simon replied kindly. "I'm Simon, and this is Aaron."

"Very good," he said eagerly. "I'm headed to meet up with my Lord, Jesus of Nazareth, and then—"

"Wait, wait. Did you say Jesus of Nazareth?" Simon interrupted. "We were about to invite him to dinner."

"Praise the Lord! You are certainly in the right place at the right time!" Bartimaeus shouted with gusto. "I'm one of his followers. I would be glad to pass on the invitation."

"Thank you, Bartimaeus," Simon said with a smile. "Since we are traveling together, can you tell us about him?"

"I thought you'd never ask," he replied. "Let me tell you my story. Before I met Jesus, my life was terrible. One day I got sick and slowly went blind. The priests thought I committed some horrible sin, as did my family. I searched my heart and confessed my sins, only to remain blind. I lost everything. Once I made a decent living as a respected salesman, mainly in wheat and olives. I spent most of my money on doctors, but they couldn't fix my sight. With no work or money, my family abandoned me. I grew bitter. The only thing left to do was beg. I was determined not to be an ordinary beggar; I was going to be the best beggar Jericho had ever seen! Plus, I had one thing going for me—my loud voice. People tell me that if I were alive during Joshua's time, the Lord wouldn't have needed to help bring down the walls of Jericho. My voice alone could have done the trick!"

"I can see that," I said with amusement toward the jolly traveler.

"One day rumor had it that Jesus of Nazareth was coming through town," Bartimaeus explained. "They said he was a miracle worker. I was pretty skeptical, but when you're blind, you can't be too picky. I sat on the side of the road outside Jericho with my cloak to keep the money people tossed my way. Jesus was coming, and the people didn't want the good teacher to be pestered by a poor beggar like me. I'm a persistent fellow, as you may have gathered, so when the crowd began to roar, I knew it was my chance. 'Jesus, Son of David, have mercy on me!'[82] I shouted. I kept shouting, which annoyed the crowd, but I didn't care. Then he called me over to him. I left my cloak on the roadside because I knew my begging days were over. Next Jesus asked me, 'What do you want me to do for you?' I said, 'My teacher, let me see again.'"[83]

Bartimaeus stopped and his eyes grew large. "Do you know what happened next?" he said. "Jesus said to me, 'Go; your faith has made you well.'[84] That's right, he said my faith had made me well. I never thought I had that much faith. Now I gladly follow him like a sheep because he is the Good Shepherd, after all."

"We have heard that," Simon snapped with sarcasm.

"Following Jesus," Bartimaeus continued, not seeming to notice, "that was the best decision I ever made, that's for sure!"

As Bartimaeus spoke, I hung on every word. "Please tell me more about his teachings," I said.

"Oh, he's the real deal," he continued. "When he prays, he prays to his Father. That means a lot to me. My father, Timaeus, loved me when I was successful, but when I became a beggar, he cast me aside. Jesus reminded me that my true father is not found on this earth. Do you know what I mean?"

"All too well," I replied. I started to speak about my father but then bit my tongue. As we continued walking, I pondered his words and fought back tears. I loved the idea of praying so personally to God.

As we finished our journey, my heart was conflicted. I could not reconcile the man who insulted the Pharisees with the man who transformed the life of Bartimaeus. I prayed every step of the way as we arrived at Simon's beautiful home.

That evening I was the only guest, but Simon proved to be a gracious host. He greeted me with a kiss and provided water to wash my feet and oil to anoint my head. We even feasted on lamb, which was a rare treat indeed. I felt unworthy of such kindness, but I celebrated with joy.

After dinner I settled in for a cozy night's sleep. The next morning, Simon was awake early once again. "I just received word," he said with enthusiasm. "Bartimaeus delivered the message. Jesus is coming for dinner in two days!"

The buzz of anticipation was so intense that I could hardly focus. Simon and his wife worked hard on the preparations. They made sure there was plenty of room for all the guests. The dining area was in a courtyard, where travelers could see our preparations.

"What's the occasion?" one man asked as he passed by.

"Simon has invited many Pharisees for dinner," I said. "Our guest of honor is a man named Jesus of Nazareth."

"I see," the stranger replied, smiling kindly. "That sounds like a holy gathering. I pray you all enjoy the evening."

His gracious words sank into my heart. Since I had not been a Pharisee for very long, I had to get used to being perceived as a holy man. After all, not long ago, nobody would have made such an assumption about me.

Soon hungry travelers arrived at the house. Dinner was prepared. Finally, I saw Jesus for the first time. As he walked over to recline at his seat, I studied his every move, searching for any clue that might help my report for Joseph. While I wanted to notice something uniquely good or evil about this man, my first impression was that he looked rather ordinary.

Unlike the previous evening, Simon didn't greet Jesus with a kiss or offer water to wash his feet or oil to anoint his head. I had never seen a guest treated so poorly, much less the guest of honor. Simon's lack of hospitality was a great insult.

As we reclined at the table, my eyes were glued to Jesus. Several minutes later, a woman nervously entered the room. Looking at her, I could tell she was a sinner. Anyone who has ever consorted in the "companions of gluttons" would notice. The way she held her eyes low to the ground while nervously clutching an alabaster jar of ointment revealed a sense of unworthiness. My heart was suddenly heavy at the memory of my own sinful past. This unwelcome guest immediately stopped the dinner conversation. Poor Simon couldn't even look at her. He knew she had already ruined the evening. What could a host do in such a situation? Everyone watched in horror as she approached Jesus. I tried to look away, but I couldn't; nobody could. Then she sat at his feet. I felt bad for Jesus. After all, the poor teacher was expecting some holy conversation about Scripture. Instead, a sinful woman had dared to enter the room and sat at his feet.

"This is unbelievable," a fellow Pharisee hissed into my ear. "Who does she think she is?"

Jesus needed bold action; otherwise, it would appear as if he approved of her sinful ways. I found myself between two Pharisees who were whispering to each other.

"She needs to repent before approaching a holy man," the first one said.

"If he is a holy man," the other replied, "he doesn't seem nearly as concerned with holiness as we are."

As I pondered their words, my heart wrestled within me. I felt the heaviness of my own unworthiness. I used to be a sinner too, but that was in my former life. She was still a sinner, still weighed down by unworthiness. We Pharisees strive to uphold the commandments while she obviously didn't. I don't like to seem superior, but if I had the chance to reform my ways, she could do it too. There's no excuse!

I hoped Jesus would quietly send her away. Perhaps he would tell her to confess her sins before following him. That seemed like an honorable solution. Instead, to the shock of everyone, he allowed her to bathe his feet with the ointment, her tears, and her hair. I was so annoyed. How could she get away with doing that?

"If this man were a prophet," Simon said, no longer able to hold himself back, "he would have known who and what kind of woman this is who is touching him—that she is a sinner."[85]

Jesus turned his gaze to the dinner host. "Simon, I have something to say to you."

"Teacher," Simon replied, "Speak."[86]

"A certain creditor had two debtors," Jesus began. "One owed five hundred denarii, and the other fifty. When they could not pay, he canceled the debts for both of them. Now which of them will love him more?"[87]

A story about two debtors was the last thing anyone expected to hear. Simon was agitated by this distraction, given the pressure of the moment. He shrugged as if to suggest he would play along with this game. "I suppose the one for whom he canceled the greater debt."

"You have judged rightly,"[88] Jesus said, nodding in agreement.

Where is he going with this? I wondered.

Next, Jesus turned his gaze to the sinful woman. "Do you see this woman? I entered your house; you gave me no water for my feet, but she has bathed my feet with her tears and dried them with her hair. You gave me no kiss, but from the time I came in she has not stopped kissing my feet. You did not anoint my head with oil, but she has anointed my feet with ointment. Therefore, I tell you, her sins, which were many, have been forgiven; hence she has shown great love. But the one to whom little is forgiven, loves little." Then he declared to the woman. "Your sins are forgiven."[89]

The room erupted in outrage. "This man is out of his mind!" the Pharisee next to me said. "Who does he think he is, forgiving sins? Only God can forgive sins."

It was the most awkward dinner I had ever attended. That entire evening troubled my heart. I could see the appeal of Jesus. He let this woman kiss his feet without recoiling in horror. Clearly, he had a heart for this sinner, but holiness demands repentance. You can't just get away with sin. You have to face the consequences, like everybody else. Jesus had no right to accept such a sinner without conditions. She gave no confession of sin, nor did she amend her ways. I confessed, and I changed under Joseph's guidance. Why should she get off so easily?

After all the guests left, Simon found me in the courtyard.

"Aaron," Simon explained, "I'm so sorry that Jesus and that sinner ruined the evening. You deserve better."

"Simon, as I looked at that sinner," I replied, "she reminded me of my past before Joseph. You see—"

"Enough," Simon interrupted. "Please don't compare yourself to her. You repented long ago while she didn't. Remember that you are a holy and righteous man now. You remind me so much of myself when I was your age."

His compliment caught me by surprise. I soaked up his affirming words. My father rarely said a kind word to me. Joseph never showered me with praise either. But Simon's words gave me confidence.

"Aaron," Simon continued, "one of my dinner companions gave me new reports about our guest of honor. Jesus told a parable about a Pharisee and a tax collector praying in the temple. Do you think the hero of this story was the holy shepherd of Israel? No. Instead, he praised a tax collector. Those rotten cheats received his adoration."

Simon had a good point. Jesus shouldn't be celebrating those sinful folks while criticizing people like us who do our best to uphold the commandments.

"Worse yet," Simon continued, "Jesus dined with the worst sinner I can imagine."

"I suppose now you're going to tell me that Jesus was dining with Zacchaeus, the chief tax collector," I said with laughter, hoping to break the tension.

"Yes, that's right." Simon replied. "How did you know?"

"I was joking. My father used to complain about how tax collectors were driving him to drink. He often threatened to march from Arimathea to Jericho and squash that little scoundrel, Zacchaeus."

Simon nodded. "I see you are starting to understand the kind of person we are dealing with in Jesus of Nazareth. He's dangerous."

I tried to imagine Jesus reclining at the table with Zacchaeus. That thought was so vile, I couldn't handle it. How could any holy person ever accept that thief as a guest? Zacchaeus had destroyed my family, and hundreds more suffered on account of his greed. His sins deserved punishment, not acceptance. I began to stew in anger.

"Don't worry. I have a plan." Simon grew excited as he explained it. "Some Pharisees are going to put the teacher to the test. Get some rest, and then we'll head to Jerusalem."

As we traveled to Jerusalem, I told Simon more about my past and my conversion. I also told him how Joseph read from Proverbs, "Those who keep the law are wise children—"

"... but companions of gluttons shame their parents,"[90] Simon finished, having also memorized these words.

Next, I shared the holy words that the Lord gave to Joshua before inheriting the Promised Land. "Only be strong and very courageous, being careful to act in accordance with all the law that my servant Moses commanded you—"

"Do not turn from it to the right hand or to the left, so that you may be successful wherever you go,"[91] Simon said, finishing for me once again. "Aaron, I'm so glad you chose this passage. I believe the Lord guided you to it for a reason. We need to follow all the laws of Moses, not just some of them. That's why Jesus is such a threat. He doesn't take the laws of Moses as seriously as we do. That is why we must put him to the test."

Soon we traveled to Jerusalem, where Jesus had a crowd. Immediately, several Pharisees and scribes brought a woman before him. She had been caught in adultery, violating the sacred law that the Lord gave to Moses. They stood her before Jesus as she stared at the ground, knowing her punishment was coming.

"Watch this," Simon whispered in my ear. "The law is clear that adultery requires her to be put to death. Either Jesus will obey the law, as your favorite passage from Joshua instructs, or he will twist the Scriptures to his own pleasing. We will soon know the truth."

As I laid eyes upon the sinful woman, I admired Simon's fierce devotion. He was upholding the laws of Moses. He smiled at me, and I swelled with pride. I lamented the decisions of that poor woman. If only she had made better choices. She had to be punished, as the Scriptures demand. She had it coming.

The scribes and Pharisees looked directly at Jesus. "Teacher," one of them said, "this woman was caught in the very act of committing adultery. Now in the law Moses commanded us to stone such women. Now what do you say?"[92]

In that defining moment, Jesus scribbled something into the sand, but I couldn't see what he had written. Everyone was waiting impatiently for him to speak. Finally, he looked up. "Let anyone among you who is without sin be the first to throw a stone at her."[93]

"I told you he was dangerous," Simon replied, gloating in relief. "We now have proof that Jesus cares more about an adulterer than defending the commandments. We gave him the opportunity to honor the law, and he failed."

"That's right. Jesus should have stuck to Scripture," I affirmed.

As we hurried away, Simon smiled with glee. "Come on. Let's go and tell Joseph right away!"

As I looked back, Jesus and the woman were still talking, but I couldn't hear their words. They were inconsequential. Jesus should have upheld the holy standards the Lord gave us. Simon was right that Jesus had twisted the Scriptures to his own pleasing.

As we traveled back to Arimathea, I was eager to see Joseph once again. Upon our arrival, he already had a fire for us, with bread, wine, olives, and figs for dinner. As always, he greeted us with a kiss and provided water for our feet and oil for our heads.

"Tell me everything you have learned about Jesus," Joseph said eagerly.

"My pleasure," Simon replied with a sly smile. "That man is more comfortable with adulterers and prostitutes than holy men. Aaron, go ahead, tell him. Did Jesus accept the teachings of Moses or not?"

"Well . . ." I began. The situation was more complex than Simon presented, but I knew I had to give a clear answer. "It's true. A woman was caught in adultery. Jesus refused to quote Scripture when put to the test."

"Is there anything good about this man?" Joseph pressed.

"Not at all," Simon insisted. "I threw him a banquet, which a sinner ruined. Yet Jesus rebuked me! Yes, me, instead of her."

"That's terrible." Joseph affirmed. We all fell silent, and then Joseph looked at Simon. "Out of curiosity, why did he rebuke you?"

"Oh." Simon's face turned red in embarrassment. "It's nothing. I just could have been a better host, that's all. What that woman did was the real scandal though!"

Joseph sensed Simon wasn't telling him the full story. Rather than argue, he poked the fire with a stick and remained silent. I was torn between these two holy men whom I admired.

"He's dangerous," Simon continued. "He doesn't love and defend the Scriptures like we do."

"Yet Jesus of Nazareth said, 'The scribes and the Pharisees sit on Moses' seat; therefore, do whatever they teach you and follow it; but do not do as they do, for they do not practice what they teach,'"[94] Joseph said. "If Jesus approves of our teachings, how can you oppose him so vigorously?"

"I'm sorry, Joseph," I interrupted with confusion. "Did you say Jesus approves of the Pharisees' teachings? I had no idea."

"That's right. It's only the actions he criticizes," Joseph said.

"See, Aaron?" Simon asserted, eager to steer the conversation in a different direction. "Joseph can't seem to grasp when he is being insulted. Jesus has called us a bunch of hypocrites, yet Joseph keeps defending him. I'm fighting to protect fine young men like you."

There was a long pause as tempers had once again flared. Simon was furious while Joseph appeared sad, gazing at the fire. Eventually, Simon explained. "Aaron, I think there's something you need to know." He paused and took a sip of wine. "Joseph once mentored a bright young man much like you. He had high hopes for him. While the man became a Pharisee, he eventually disappointed Joseph. He claimed the young man cared too much about outer appearances."

"OK," I said, not really understanding.

"Do you know who that young man was?" Simon asked.

"No, who?"

"That young man . . . was me."

"I never knew," I said staring at Simon in disbelief. Then I turned to Joseph. "Is this true?"

Joseph nodded slowly, his eyes still on the fire. "Yes, it is. Simon was the brightest young man I ever mentored. He still has great potential, but things didn't work out. Aaron, I have tried to protect you from such matters. Let's save this conversation for another day. Now we need to make preparations to go to Jerusalem for Passover. That's enough talking for tonight."

Joseph left for bed, but Simon continued to speak with me. "You did well, Aaron. Really well. I'm proud of you, and so is the Lord."

"Thanks," I said. "I didn't realize the two of you had a past."

"I know Joseph is a good man," Simon replied. "He tried his best to mentor me. The problem is, the old man never grows tired of answering one question with another question. You've probably noticed that by now." I nodded as he continued. "Jesus isn't much better. According to my sources, he's full of questions. That's the problem with folks like Joseph and Jesus. They would rather ask a question than give a direct answer. Aaron, I have the answers you seek. I know because I was once like you."

Simon's words melted my heart. While Joseph taught me many lessons, he didn't have the same eloquence or give me the clear answers I sought. Simon inspired me to defend my faith against people like Jesus.

As he poured water over the fire, the darkness reminded me of the strange yet distant feelings I had toward Joseph.

After Simon left early the next morning, I pressed Joseph for answers.

"Why didn't you tell me about Simon?"

"What makes you think I should have?"

"There you go answering a question with another question," I said with frustration. "Please just give me a straight answer."

"Why do you only seek answers?" Joseph chuckled. "I tried so hard with Simon. I taught him to see the sin within his heart, but he stopped doing that. Now he only sees the sins of others. That is where our paths went in opposite directions."

"Joseph, I came to you seeking safety."

"Does safety always come from the Lord?"

"Forget about it," I said in anger. Joseph was annoying me like never before. He wasn't taking this threat seriously. The longer we argued about Jesus and his teachings, the more tense our relationship grew.

"There's something else you should know," Joseph said, his voice tinged with dread. "The Sanhedrin is planning to trap Jesus during Passover. I'm worried that some have already made up their minds."

On the way to Jerusalem, we quietly prayed the Psalms to ourselves until arriving at that holy city on a hill. The next few days were filled with controversy. Jesus caused a stir in the Temple by debating Scripture with the authorities. Once again, he posed a bunch of questions rather than giving simple answers. I knew he would go too far. Finally, people realized how dangerous he was. Simon had been right about him the whole time.

Next, one of his disciples, Judas Iscariot, turned Jesus over to the Sanhedrin. Joseph tried to defend Jesus, but they found him guilty. The high priest, Caiaphas, confronted Jesus, asking him, "Are you the Messiah, the Son of the Blessed One?"[95]

To my horror, Jesus claimed to be the Messiah. This confession revealed his delusions and sealed his fate. To protect Israel from danger, they had to get rid of this man. This chain of events continued until Pilate ordered Jesus to be crucified.

The death of Jesus left me with mixed emotions. I was relieved that this false teacher would no longer be a thorn in our side. However, his death meant his crazy followers venerated him as some kind of a martyr.

What happened next changed my life forever. Joseph shamefully went to Pilate and asked for his body. Pilate agreed. What's worse, Joseph was not alone. Another Pharisee, a man named Nicodemus, joined in this devious act of betrayal. He brought myrrh and aloe, and together they buried Jesus in a tomb. How dare they give this false teacher an honorable burial! It was so shameful! This revealed my deepest fears about Joseph. He was not just sympathetic to Jesus; he was following him!

I left Jerusalem alone, crying nearly the entire way back to Arimathea.

Several days later Joseph came running through town. The sight of an old man running was so shameful that the kids in town all laughed at him. He didn't care. Joseph ran right up to me. "Aaron!" he exclaimed. "The most wonderful thing happened. Jesus is alive! He has risen!"

"Oh, Joseph," I said with a deep sigh. "Remember that day in the synagogue when you changed my life? You read the following words, 'Those who keep the law are wise children, but companions of gluttons shame their parents.'[96] Yet you don't even believe those words anymore. Jesus preferred the companionship of shameful people. I guess you are joining them."

"Aaron," Joseph insisted, "Jesus is alive!"

"Oh, Joseph," I said in grief, "you were once so distinguished and honorable. You were the father I never had. Jesus turned you into a crazy lunatic spouting embarrassing tall tales."

I turned my back on him, my heart unable to bear looking at him. I'm still haunted by the memory of his appearance. He had such wild eyes. This was no longer the mentor I once admired. As I walked away, my heart was broken once more. I knew at that moment that I had lost not one father but two.

Years have passed since these events took place. I'm still a Pharisee living in Arimathea. Simon visits often, and we've become great friends. Joseph joined a band of fishermen, prostitutes, and tax collectors who continue to believe in this kingdom of God. Joseph's fall from grace was complete. The man who saved me from the wrong kind of people spent the rest of his days hanging out with those same people.

Jesus of Nazareth threatened the two things I held dearest in life: the Scriptures and my relationship with Joseph. While I lost Joseph, I continue to stand firm in defense of Scripture. Thanks to Simon, I have the support I need.

Joseph and Nicodemus weren't the only Pharisees seduced by his lies. One man is a particular threat these days. His name is Saul of Tarsus. He was once a model Pharisee, defending everything holy and sacred, until he fell from grace. Now he travels great distances to follow the misguided teachings of Jesus—and to mislead many along the way. He needs to be stopped. Otherwise, more of the good sheep of Israel will be led astray by the man who falsely claimed to be the "Good Shepherd."

If Jesus could destroy the faith of holy men such as Joseph, Nicodemus, and Saul, then the rest of us are also in great danger. People occasionally ask for my thoughts about Jesus of Nazareth and his death. I don't always have a good answer. Here is what I can say with conviction: I wish Jesus of Nazareth had never lived!

Conclusion

THE STORIES TOLD BY Deborah, Shem, Sarah, Max, and Aaron force us to consider their side of the controversial story about Jesus of Nazareth. Whether we realize it or not, even if we claim to be followers of Jesus, at times his presence threatens our deeply held values including social status, biblical interpretation, patriotism, wealth, family, and more. Even the most loyal followers of Jesus can become his enemies, often without realizing it. Although it may have been uncomfortable at times, I hope these stories have served as a sort of mirror to help you see yourself more clearly in relation to your faith, your heart, and, most of all, Jesus.

These five stories will likely provoke divergent reactions. Some readers may feel their values are under attack while others may welcome the chance to consider new perspectives and deepen their faith. Some may resent this effort to reimagine the biblical narratives while others may gain new insights about the gospels. Some may hate the suggestion that they could have killed Jesus while others may do some soul searching to consider that possibility. Any faith that is worthwhile must be open to challenge. One of the hardest things to do in life is to listen to an opposing viewpoint with which one strongly disagrees, but true love of enemies requires doing exactly that.

What if Deborah, Shem, Sarah, Max, and Aaron are still speaking today? Do you see them on TV, debate with them on social media, or hear them on the radio? Do you meet them at work, at school, or even in church? Do you hear their voices in political speeches, in conversations with friends, or from loved ones at the dinner table? Most importantly, do you hear their voices, whispering to your heart?

I do. They haunt me with an uncomfortable possibility. Had I lived in the time of Jesus, I would have killed him. Maybe, just maybe, you might have too.

Endnotes

1. John 19:6 (New Revised Standard Version; all subsequent citations are from this version).
2. Matt 26:22
3. Matt 5:44
4. Exod 10:3
5. Luke 12:49, 51
6. Matt 11:28
7. Matt 5:4
8. John 11:21
9. John 11:28
10. John 11:32
11. John 11:36
12. John 11:37
13. John 11:39
14. John 11:39
15. John 11:40
16. John 11:43
17. Matt 21:9
18. Matt 22:29
19. Matt 26:52–53
20. Eccl 3:1
21. Eccl 3:8
22. Exod 10:3
23. John 18:36
24. Luke 23:18
25. Matt 27:29
26. Luke 23:42
27. Luke 23:43
28. Matt 4:19
29. Mark 1:25
30. Mark 2:5
31. Mark 2:11

32. Mark 2:12
33. Luke 9:12
34. Luke 9:13
35. John 6:48
36. John 6:56
37. John 6:52
38. Mark 10:43–44
39. Luke 9:23
40. Luke 18:22
41. Mark 11:9
42. Matt 26:5
43. Matt 27:42
44. John 19:30
45. Ps 118:24
46. Prov 22:6
47. John 1:46
48. Isa 9:1
49. Luke 2:48
50. Luke 2:49
51. Prov 17:6
52. Isa 61:1–2
53. Isa 61:5, 7
54. Ps 126:5
55. Luke 4:18
56. Luke 4:21
57. Luke 4:22
58. Luke 4:25–26
59. Luke 4:27
60. Lev 24:16
61. Prov 26:11
62. Luke 7:9
63. Prov 29:3
64. Mark 3:34–35
65. Matt 5:3
66. Matt 6:9–10
67. Matt 5:41
68. Matt 8:6
69. Matt 8:7
70. Matt 8:8–9
71. Matt 8:10
72. Mark 12:14 "Caesar" used instead of "Emperor" for emphasis.
73. Mark 12:17
74. Matt 10:34
75. John 11:50
76. Matt 27:54

77. Prov 28:7
78. Josh 1:7
79. Luke 11:39–40
80. Matt 23:24, 27
81. Ps 14:1; 53:1
82. Mark 10:47
83. Mark 10:51
84. Mark 10:52
85. Luke 7:39
86. Luke 7:40
87. Luke 7:41–42
88. Luke 7:43
89. Luke 7:44–48
90. Prov 28:7
91. Josh 1:7
92. John 8:4-5
93. John 8:7
94. Matt 23:2–3
95. Mark 14:61
96. Prov 28:7

CPSIA information can be obtained
at www.ICGtesting.com
Printed in the USA
LVHW050023170921
698020LV00007B/18

9 781666 711561